T0303616

ASPIRING

Damien Wilkins

ANNUALink

For James Archie Hughes

1.

Pete's was where I had an after-school job. There was no one at the restaurant called Pete. The owner's name was Garth but he hadn't got around to changing the name. He didn't want to climb on a ladder and paint it up. 'Besides,' Garth said, 'who'd want to come to a place called Garth's? Sounds like someone clearing his throat.'

I wouldn't have needed a ladder.

I'd almost finished my three-hour shift, 5–8 p.m. I'd chipped the candle wax off the vacant tables, mopped the storeroom floor, changed a blown bulb in the toilets, and was just about done cleaning the meat freezer of its little frozen puddles of blood, inside which were old labels: sirloin x 2, rump x 3, roo stew. It was like a murder scene at Scott Base.

As I worked, bent over the freezer, I had sentences spooling inside my head. *Slowly it dawned on him that these icy pouches contained not next month's dinner but the neatly sliced remains of the missing scientist.* Recently I'd become aware that I had a sort of internal running commentary, looping language I couldn't turn off. Last week by the lake, I biked past a group of tourists emerging from their China Star Adventure bus and I was stuck for ages with this: *The selfie stick carried in its tip the most powerful poison on earth, but how could he prove it?* Maybe everyone had the same thing going on. Just thoughts, Ricky, was what my mum said when I mentioned it to her. But these were more than thoughts, weren't they?

I was a vegetarian but I kept that quiet at Pete's. *He was a vegetarian but no one liked vegetarians.*

In the three months I'd been working there, Garth had chewed through four kitchen hands. He was not a vegetarian. I'd found one of them—a guy called Will—crying at the rear entrance when I was putting out the rubbish. 'I'm gonna get that fat pig,' said Will.

Will was nineteen, an ex-snowboarder with a busted knee. He'd been in line to go to the Winters or the X Games or something. Until he crashed out. I lived in a town of dudes in moon boots. Kids on crutches.

Will was about 5'8". I couldn't stop estimating people's heights. It was another tic in my head. I'd mentally chalk up everyone I met.

I was 6'7". And more, a little each month, each week, each day. Technically I was probably growing in the very moment I was thinking about growing. Or not thinking about growing. I slept curled up, like an extremely long foetus. *The coiled and sleeping snake is not feared for its ability to strike instantly but for its capacity to unfurl endlessly, revealing its length inch by terrifying inch.*

I had to lean over Will to tip out the rubbish. 'Hey, man!' said Will. 'Watch the jacket, Big Bird.' The next day Will would be gone.

'Where there's a will,' said Garth, 'there's a way.'

My job was also to help out in the kitchen with the prep. Logan (5'10"), the most junior kitcheneer, had shown me how to cut onions, slice carrots, and do it fast, without fear of losing a finger. The height of the bench was wrong and I got a sore back but I didn't tell anyone. Most of me was sore: my neck, my hamstrings, my long feet pressing against the ends of my socks, my strained shoes. I was like the Hulk, always bursting the confines. But a skinny Hulk. Also I had to run errands. I had to reach up to the top shelf for Garth, who was short, not even 5'6", though he had heels on his shoes and a self-expanding manner. Maybe *he* was the true Hulk. With his belly, he tried to appear taller, or longer. It moved in front of him like a ship's prow, clearing a space, making waves.

Thinking about him summoned him. Garth came over and stared at the piles of meat I'd stacked, pushing his forefinger into a few of them. He put his nose down to one pack, then picked it up and lobbed it across the kitchen, where Dave, his second-in-command, turned and caught it. They hadn't spoken.

Garth peered inside the freezer, inspecting my work. 'Get all these back in there smartly,' he said.

'Yes, Garth,' I said.

He hiffed another meat pack at Dave's back. Somehow Dave (6'1") spun and grabbed it, reverse-cup style. Dave played cricket for North Otago. Garth went 'Hmpff' and walked out of the kitchen.

Garth had a line of sweat almost permanently on his upper lip. His shirt was marked with wet moons under the arms and jagged stains across his back—yeah, okay, like the mountain range looming over our little town. When Garth sat on his stool in the kitchen, you couldn't see the stool. It was part of him, like another leg. If anyone else thought of resting his weary bones ('weary boner' as Dave liked to say) on that stool, he got an egg flying at him or a bagel frisbeed at his head.

Garth was explosive, your typical chef, I suppose—a hurler of wet cloths, balled and leaden, and insults. But he was all right to me. I was the youngest on the payroll. One time he said to me

9

at the end of the day, 'You're a good kid, Ricky. Don't go wrong. Don't blow it.'

'I won't,' I said. I'd found a ten-dollar note on the floor by his office and I'd handed it in. This struck him as odd.

'Don't hang around a kitchen too long.'

'I like it.' It was true.

'I don't want to hear you say that.' Garth trod his cigarette into the ground, mashing it with his shoe. He never lit his cigarettes—he'd given up smoking years before apparently, but he couldn't live without the feel of it on his lips. I swept these mangled unsmoked ciggies. I was sweeping up a fortune.

In fact, I liked the sweeping and I liked the buzz, the meshing of working parts, the steam, the behind-the-scenes. I liked cutlery, crockery, the fit of a lid on a pot and the way the lid lifted slightly as things came to the boil. I liked things boiling. Would someone please turn the temperature up on this life of mine?

Garth wasn't having a bar of it. 'Anyone comes to me and says I want to be part of the industry, I say, if you have any other options, explore them. Deeply. It'll eat your soul, Ricky. In a kitchen you think you're doing the cooking. Reality is the kitchen is cooking you. Understand?'

I didn't understand but I nodded. I didn't understand anything, beginning with those saliva cigarettes.

The meat packs were back in the freezer. I tied a full plastic bag of rubbish shut and took it out the rear entrance. Mr Le Clair's Cadillac was parked across the street. The driver's door was open and the chauffeur, in his sunglasses, had one foot down on the street while the rest of him stayed inside. This manoeuvre meant he was at least 6'2". From the car came a faint spooky kind of music. Mr Le Clair must have entered by the front door, like a punter. But he wasn't a punter.

I went back inside Pete's and heard Garth calling my name.

Mr Le Clair wasn't from round here. Was he American? Googling didn't turn up much. Someone said he might be Garth's financial backer, a silent partner in Pete's. But why invest in Pete's? Surely there were better options. Lots of Yanks were buying up land around Aspiring. Helicopters flew over the town, depositing these rich-listers on remote hilltops where their low-roofed mansions were inserted into the landscape, harmonious, grey and slatey, with infinity pools like fallen mirrors. Most of the cargo on these flights was golf clubs and fly-fishing gear. The wine cellars were already stocked; the imported chefs were already at work. Sergio. Philippe. Mr Hua. My friend Sim's father flew for Aspiring Air. One time he couriered a grand piano up Mount Aspiring, swinging it into place six thousand feet up for some dude's birthday singalong.

Mr Le Clair didn't appear to be one of these chopper folk. Way too seedy and way too connected to Garth. His voice was weird as well, as though *he* couldn't decide where he came from. Maybe he's a vampire, Rachel said. She was the longest-serving waitress. We only see him, she said, when the sun's gone down. Mr Le Clair was certainly pale, with hooded eyes, and though his cheeks were without stubble, they always carried shadows of growth as though ink was washing just under the skin along his jaw. He spoke quickly and you never saw his teeth. Out of earshot of Garth, Logan said Le Clair was some kind of drug guy. You don't know that, Dave said. Look at his nose, Logan said. That's your classic coke nose. The nostrils cave in and the surgeons make a new one but it never looks right. He's a bad man. Stay clear, Ricky. Rachel laughed. What's he going to do to Ricky? Drink his blood? Fresh meat, laughed Logan. He went to pinch my arm but I dodged him. Get off, I said.

The car was definitely from 'the place once called America', as Dad referred to it. But this was no ordinary long black Cadillac. This was a short black Cadillac. There was no other way of describing it. The car was a Caddy in every respect—and bore the maker's name—but it was missing several feet in length. The bonnet, or what once-were-Americans called the hood, was severely shortened. Could the engine even fit in there? And likewise the boot (trunk) was a sort of sawn-off number. Dave, who knew something about cars, said it was a kind of outrage this Caddy, like a kid's Caddy, something that got made at fantastic expense for the spoiled son of the world's richest, stupidest man. You imagined it getting wrapped in crêpe paper and finished off with a big black bow. Happy birthday, Doofus! Happy birthday, Donald!

It was the second year of Trump's presidency. Everything was stupid. *As the president spoke today, healthy birds dropped out of the sky.*

'Come through to the back,' Garth told me.

In the office, Mr Le Clair, thin and about the same age as my dad, looked me up and down. He was smoking a cigar. He was actually smoking it, though smoking of course was banned on the premises. The smell was of dog shit but from a very expensive dog. 'What are you feeding the boy, Garth? Donuts?'

'There you go,' said Garth.

'Then how is it you're that shape, Garth?' said Mr Le Clair.

The frier had made Garth's skin shiny and yellow. His fingernails, though, were astonishingly clean—like a girl's—with pink cuticles. One time a health inspector came and told Garth he had to wear a paper hat when he was cooking. He had to wear plastic gloves. 'What am I,' said Garth, 'a surgeon?'

Garth *was* a little medical, I thought. There was nothing he protected more jealously than his knives. They weren't stuck in a block—like Mum had at home—they were wrapped in a leather apron. If any idiot tried washing Garth's knives, he may as well not show up the next day. 'A knife washed is a knife ruined,' Garth said. You *wiped* a knife clean on a special cloth. When Garth unwrapped his apron of knives and looked at them in their individual pockets, then folded them up again, he may have been dealing with a baby on a change mat he was so tender and careful.

Garth had a daughter who was about my age. He would always bring her up as a way of suggesting how far we all had to go to meet a reasonable standard as workers. His daughter was always quicker, neater, more powerful, more intelligent than us. The trouble was the daughter lived with Garth's ex-wife in Auckland, a place no one could mention without Garth emitting a low growl. Grrrraucklarrrggghhhnd. Occasionally the ex-wife called him at Pete's and that was terrible for everyone. From the office we could all hear him. On those days Garth was rude even to the customers if they so much as questioned whether the ham roll came with mustard.

I put my hands in my pockets. My hands were huge; they were unknown to me.

'Hey, kid,' said Mr Le Clair, 'you're blocking the light. You're blocking the sun.'

'Go stand against the wall,' Garth told me.

Here's the thing: Garth had a height chart going, marking off my progress. It had started in week two of my employment, when Logan pointed out I was still growing and pretty soon I wouldn't fit in the kitchen. I'd bumped my head on the edge of a high cupboard. Garth had put the chart up for his daughter, who would apparently come down to Aspiring during school holidays.

For fun Garth asked me to stand beside the chart, which only went up to six feet. His daughter's measurements were from years ago. Keri, aged five years and seven months. Keri, aged eight years and two months. Etcetera. He asked Logan to stand on a chair and they marked off another foot above the chart with a tape measure. Somehow Mr Le Clair had got interested—he'd seen the fresh marks on the wall in Garth's office. Now the only time they measured me was when Mr Le Clair was present. It was a thing. I didn't get it at first. Two adults curious about my height to this extent. Sure, I could have walked away at any point. Was this the sort of thing Garth had warned me about?

The second time Mr Le Clair came and they marked off my progress, I got it. They were betting on my growth. For how much money, I didn't know. But whoever won had to give me a cut—their idea. This wasn't something I reported to anyone. They'd slip me twenty dollars as I left the office. They may as well have been betting on a flea race. On how long they could go without blinking. People are weird.

I stood there and Garth reached up with a pen. He couldn't quite do it this day so Mr Le Clair kicked the stool over and Garth stood on that. No one kicked the stool.

'Soon that's a ladder job,' said Mr Le Clair, who was average height. He wore a dark suit and a white shirt and a string tie. On the lapel of his suit he had a tiny silver pin in a kind of arrow shape, but I'd never got close enough to see exactly what it was. He carried a black cane with a silver tip. His boots were black and ended in a sharp point. His hair bore comb-marks, wavy ridges that glistened with some kind of oily substance. The hair didn't move a hair. And there was that ruined nose, just a thin slash, really. Had he been something in the music business? The manager of someone promising, dead at twenty-seven? Or had he himself been that promising person? A few inches from a breakthrough before bad luck struck? I knew about bad luck. I knew how it could reach out and in a moment rearrange everything.

'Another quarter inch,' announced Garth. He was unhappy about this. He'd lost the bet again.

'You got tall parents, kid?' said Mr Le Clair.

'His father's same as me,' said Garth. 'Just a little bigger.'

Mr Le Clair was always trying to figure out the secret. 'Brothers and sisters?'

'There's just me,' I said.

I hadn't told anyone at Pete's about Mike. I liked to keep Mikey private; he was mine. Never again would I show anyone that softball glove with my brother's name on it.

'Look at the shoes on the kid!' said Mr Le Clair. 'Your poor mother. Though there'd be advantages. You can reach for the high stuff for her, right?'

I nodded.

'Soon you'll be buying booze for your buddies.'

'Which would be illegal,' said Garth.

'Totally,' said Le Clair. 'But there'll be pressure. Still, you'll be able to look after yourself. People will want to have a go.'

'What people?' said Garth. 'What are you trying to scare the boy for?'

'He's not scared. I'm saying some squat piece of muscle will want to bring down the big house. There are people walking around with the stature and the IQ of bowling balls. Their entire *raison d'être* is—' he looked at me '—to take out pins.'

'We don't know what you're talking about,' said Garth. 'And anyway, he's got to stop growing one day.'

'In the meantime,' said Mr Le Clair, 'I keep taking your money.'

'Pardon me,' I said, 'may I go now?' I didn't care to be under the gaze of Mr Le Clair. I stood in the room and got measured so I didn't end up losing my job. Hell, this was part of my job—they paid me, didn't they?

Another thing: when they measured me and when I was in Mr Le Clair's presence, my head was clear of commentary. Le Clair seemed to suck it from me. No sentences were looping. I was blank.

'Sure, go,' said Garth. 'I'm growing chilly in your shade.'

Mr Le Clair dropped ash from his cigar onto a plate and looked me up and down one last time before turning away. He extended an arm towards me and I reached for the note: a fifty.

Garth pushed me from the room. At the door he said, 'I don't need you any more today. Go home, Ricky.' I said I hadn't quite finished all my jobs but Garth waved his hand. 'Out, go on now. You cost me enough already.' I still held the fifty-dollar note in my hand. Garth looked at it. 'Put it in your pocket. It's yours. Though I wouldn't advertise your good fortune, eh.'

Biking home, this: *He squinted against the cigar smoke. Smokescreen, he thought. But smoke … smoke, as his Auntie Rena once sang in nightclubs around the world … gets in your eyes. Your eyes water. Then what? Maybe a drop of moisture sliding over your eyeball magnifies the world and you start to see things.*

2.

I worked Tuesday, Wednesday, Friday at Pete's. That Thursday after school, I biked to the retirement village up behind the golf course where Mum was a member and Dad hated to go. It was Mum's idea that I try the village. She gave me names. 'Say you're Michelle's son,' she told me, 'and Ricky, when you walk into their places, find a seat. Don't ... loom. A lot of these people are shrinking. They don't want you looming.'

I did as I was told. Knocked on doors. Said I was Michelle's son. Crouched low and quickly found a seat. Everyone said yes. Well, first they said, What is this again? Can you explain it to me one more time? What do I have to do?

I went over it again. Our English teacher, Miss Clarke, had read about the idea of the human library—people being borrowed instead of books. Our task: find some interesting people (and everyone is interesting!), help them craft a brief story about their lives (but this is not about self-promotion), set up a 'library', invite borrowers/readers to choose a person/book. Lending time to be set at, say, ten minutes. It was a way of connecting people. A walk in someone else's shoes. Think about prejudices. Discrimination. Find the people whose stories are not often heard. Homeless people were especially good, Miss Clarke told us. But that, she added, required care and sensitivity. She looked around at her class. Maybe, she said, stay away from the homeless. We don't have homeless people in Aspiring, someone said. Hmm, said our teacher. At that moment I thought of Tessa Thompson, who lived with her mother in a caravan on a vacant section above Beacon Point. Not homeless, but it was rumoured they washed in the lake after dark. I glanced across the room at Angus Dean, 5'8". He and Tessa were linked. Angus was bouncing his powerful legs up and down. He was our basketball team's best forward and constantly surprised with his leap. In speaking his name, he was also using one more syllable than his normal speech allowed. Angus was repeating NCEA level 2. His nickname on court was Achieved. But his fame now rested elsewhere. As of a week ago, he and Tessa Thompson were the new King and Queen of Sticky Forest. They'd replaced a year 13 couple who, it was rumoured, wanted their crown back. But was that in the constitution? Surely the monarchy could only be passed on to first-timers. The king is dead, long live the king!

When would I wear the crown?

As if hearing my thoughts, Angus put up his hand. We all turned to look at this hand, connected to this arm, his trunk, which had been involved with Tessa Thompson in the tangle and in the dark folds, the low scrubby bushes of Sticky Forest. Only Tessa wasn't looking. She continued to stare at her desk.

'Yes, Angus?' said Miss Clarke.

'Do we need a library card? I don't have one,' said Angus.

'Fucking hell,' said someone at the back of the room.

'That will not be the kind of language we have in this class,' said Miss Clarke. She was newish in Aspiring. Probably she was the only person in the room who didn't know about the King and Queen of Sticky Forest. Although maybe she did.

What else would teachers of teenagers talk about if not our love lives, our soily secrets? When they looked at us, probably they saw animals, themselves years before. Still, they had to keep up the pretence that we were receptive and eager to learn, grow, become something other than what they knew us to be. Miss Clarke told Angus he wouldn't need a library card for this exercise.

Jack Grant put up his hand. 'Usually,' Jack said, 'Angus likes exercise, Miss.'

We erupted. It had been named. Or almost. Miss Clarke changed colour.

'All right, all right,' she said.

Tessa was hunched lower now, the parting in her hair arrowing straight into her desk, but then she too glanced up and was grinning.

Once peace was restored, Miss Clarke went over the details again and told us that we'd set up the human library at the Aspiring fair in a few weeks. There'd be a marquee tent, signage. Find your people, she told us. Address the prejudices of this place. We want diversity.

Jack Grant put up his hand again. 'Put down your hand,' Miss Clarke said. Sarah Lovell put up her hand. Miss Clarke asked if it was a serious question.

'I think so,' said Sarah. Miss Clarke nodded.

'Is diverse more Māori? Do we need to find a Māori?'

'Ryan's half Māori, Miss,' said Alex Beehan.

'Fuck off,' said Ryan.

'Okay, I thought we decided about the language in this classroom,' said Miss Clarke.

'Chinese are diverse,' said Astrid Phillips.

Kathy Wang stared straight ahead. Then I watched as she

picked up her pencil case in her mouth. Her white teeth gripped its zip.

'Listen,' said our teacher, 'I'm not going to tell you how to engage with this project. Use your brains. This is all about being as inclusive as we can be. I'm not saying who's in and who's out.'

'In and out,' said Jack Grant. 'Hear that, Angus? In and out.' Then we all laughed some more.

I looked out the window at what was always called by any visitor to the school a million-dollar view. The mountains seemed higher some days, closer, as if they were growing and not us, and one day we would look out and they would be there, accusingly, having crossed the now-dry lakebed. *You, we want a word with you.*

I'd tried first at Pete's. There was a prejudice against people who worked in hospo, right?

'Dave, would you like to be in my human library?'

I could see that the word library made him wince. 'Nah, mate, not me.'

I asked Logan, who just laughed loudly as if I'd told a great joke and then threw a wet cloth at my head. He didn't have Garth's arm.

I was too scared to ask Garth.

Rachel paused with her tray, listened very hard, and then told me she never read books.

'But this isn't about books. It'd just be you, telling your story.'

'What story?' She was setting the tables.

'Your story,' I said. 'Like, your life.'

'Who to?'

'Anyone who wants to borrow you.'

'Borrow me? Some dirty bloke is going to borrow me, is he?'

'No,' I said. 'It'll be nice.' But then I thought how do we screen for dirty blokes who want to hang with Rachel? She was mid-twenties, with a huge smile, and she earned very good tips. Someone had once put a 't' in place of the 'p' on the tips jar by the cash register.

'Nice?' She smiled at me, kind. 'Okay, leaving out the weirdos ... I'm telling my life to a stranger? Why am I doing this?'

'To connect with people,' I told her, parroting my teacher. 'Fight misunderstanding. Aid social cohesion. Offer a walk in someone else's shoes.'

'You're a funny guy, Ricky.' Then she went off to get more serviettes.

At the village (prejudice against old people), Mr Wilson was last on my list. He'd retired to Aspiring from Christchurch, where he'd been some kind of council water-care expert. He quickly agreed to join my library but he had a question: 'If I'm a book, where's my barcode, young man? What's my number in the Dewey decimal system? Eh? Eh?'

Biking home I had that buzzing in my head. The Dewey decimal system. The combination was growing stranger and stranger. This was also how words often went inside the upstairs room of my brain—they collided into nonsense. Dewy libraries. Once, I remembered, I heard a scream from the bathroom, then swearing. My mum, having her bath, had dropped her library book into the water. *Maximum* Dewey decimal system!

Then I was thinking of the dew on grass and those cold mornings of my single season of rugby. *When the ball landed, it skidded across the grass like a dinner plate skimmed over a frozen lake.* Right then I would have loved to skim a dinner plate across a frozen lake—who wouldn't?—but when was that going to happen? Climate change was cooking our lake. Last summer the water was 21 degrees, warmer for weeks on end. The lake wasn't yet in view from my bike. Usually, normally—what was normal now?—it was cold and stayed cold, fed by the Southern Alps. But even in the good old days it never froze. Froze the blood maybe, looking at it sometimes under dark clouds, the water turned gun-grey, bottomless and hostile, keeper of bodies.

What bodies?

Two summers ago a medical student from Otago tried to cross over to Jade Island on an inflatable flamingo. He captained a pink drinks tray right to the invisible bottom. I remember his parents came to town for a memorial service. They were photographed for the paper, hand-in-hand, looking out over the lake where their son was lost forever. I found Mum crying over the paper that morning. She quickly stood up and moved to the sink when I came in but I knew that she was upset. Lost sons.

My dad never looked at the lake. Seldom was out on it. Was it because of his navy days? Did he think this body of water unworthy of attention compared to the vast open seas of his youth? *The vast open seas of his youth*—my God, these were the phrases I made in my mind, turning them over again and again but never speaking them out loud. One day would that happen? I'd blurt this rubbish and people would know me for the freak I was, inside and out. Whatever. My dad drove the lakeside road with his head fixed straight as a showroom dummy. Mum would say stuff like, 'Eeeler's Point is the place to be today. Look at those whitecaps.' And Dad might grunt, never shifting his eyes from the road.

The tourists who came and took pictures of the lake, who

selfied the hell out of the whole enterprise, did they sense it, too? The Japanese. The Chinese. Germans by the truck-load. Defecating French. There was one on TV last week, squatting over a kayak. Did those precious visitors look out across the lake towards the mountains and think in their deepest selves, their deepest selfies, is this really so great? I was expecting something just a little more … *majestique*, *terrifique*, the snowy peaks a bit better defined, the surrounding hills less bare, the lake more … lakey. Were they saying, in all their languages, Aspiring is good but Queenstown is better?

Poor kayaker who found that wee gift in his vessel. *C'est diabolique.*

Still, the rich-listers continued to come, chiselling their homes from the rock. It was a quick hop over the Crown Range for all the golfing they wanted. Was that it?

People always said, Wait till they discover Aspiring. Or, It's coming, you know. It's coming. You wait.

Our town motto. Aspiring: you wait.

I couldn't wait. Suddenly I was sick of waiting.

I stood up off the seat of the bike and put in some big lunges to carry me up the final rise of the hill. Mental note: adjust seat upwards again. I'd grown — surely not in the time I'd biked to the retirement village! Would it never stop? Garth would continue losing his money.

Mental note #2: the moment you turn sixteen, get your damn driving licence, fool! Sim had his restricted and the occasional use of his mum's car.

Finally I crested the slope, the wind off the mountains struck me in the face, and the lake was there.

'It's a fine day where I am but how's the weather up there?' Old Mr Wilson had tried to touch my head but I swayed out of reach.

'Heh,' I said. 'Humf.'

I remembered what Miss Milton had said when I asked if she would like to be part of my human library: 'Oh, I can be one of your books, Ricky, but I'm not sure about my shelf life.'

Every room I entered—and ducked while entering—there'd be a gasp or a joke. 'Eiffel Tower,' someone said. 'Mind your noggin, young man!' (Prejudice against the overly tall.) Miss Milton alone made no mention of my height but then she had a special connection to our family.

Let me now measure my family.

Mum was 5'3" on her bare feet—and she was on her feet most hours. She worked in the spa and tanning clinic and on weekends she was a volunteer visitor at the retirement village. Her voluntary work was my key to getting into the houses of the village's unsuspecting residents. But I too had been a visitor. When I was small she often had me on her knee when she called on her people. She said I was there to brighten the corners. 'Because,' she also said, 'everyone liked the generation two along from their own.'

My dad was a belligerent and wide 5'9", ex-navy, ran a garage in town, was a volunteer firefighter, a decorated man. He used to call me Snicko. Ricky Ricko Snicko—I don't get it either. Years ago he'd won a bravery award for going into an inferno to save two trapped women, an elderly mother and her adult daughter. Every Christmas after that, the women came round with fruit cake and a bottle and everyone got very happy. 'I swear,' Dad told them, 'I can still smell the smoke coming off of you!' And everyone laughed, the mother and daughter hardest of all. Miss Milton was that daughter. Sometimes with other people in the house, I saw a different side of my father—more social, funny, looser.

On these occasions I always had to agree to sit on old Mrs Milton's knee. She had very sturdy knees, covered in thick tights even in hot weather. It was like perching on the wooden arms of curly chairs. This was before I started to grow.

Everything in my life is dated from before and after I started to grow. Before and after I sat on knees. Before and after I started being measured by Mr Le Clair in the back room at Pete's.

Suddenly I was above my friends, above my dad, who didn't call me Snicko any more—the name was yet another thing I'd outgrown.

The ground was farther and farther away from me, the world was receding. And I lived in the town of Aspiring, guarded by the mountains, gifted a warming lake, where French tourists freedom-camped all over us. Where the Chinese marched to photograph our famous drowned tree and their brides stood ankle deep in the water with the setting sun making their white wedding gowns translucent. Where the wealthy were gathering in flight, building perches high above our lake, awaiting some cataclysm, grouped around their grand pianos for a final singalong in the softening snow and the melting ice.

3.

At home I went immediately to the fridge and compiled some cheese and tomato sandwiches with an inch-thick blanket of mayonnaise. Then I lay on the couch in front of TV and ate them. Mum and Dad weren't home. At some point I fell asleep with the TV buzzing in my brain. Darts. One hundred and eighhhhhhhhhhhhhhty!

I had a dream that was nothing to do with anything but here it is. It's my belief that a dream shared is a dream gone and you can have it for free, no backs. I was walking along a street, kind of our neigbourhood but not quite. A dog came up to me and said, 'Can you point me in the direction of home?' Wow, a talking dog, but in the dream it was completely normal.

'Where do you live?' I said.

'Well,' said the dog, 'I was hoping you'd know me.'

I see, I said to myself inside the dream, the dog and me are having a conversation.

The dog had breath that smelled of peppermint. Mmm, I thought, this dog has heard of dog breath and has taken remedial action. Then I thought Mike had a dog. Maybe this is my brother's dog. There were photos of Mikey with his dog. One of the things we remembered every 30th of October—Mikey's day—was Mikey hiding the dog when it was just a pup in his dresser drawer so it wouldn't be found and put in the laundry overnight. After Mike died they gave the dog away. No one could bear it padding around the house looking for Mikey.

I was just about to read the tag on the dog's collar …

Then I woke up and Mum was standing above me. I was so mad to be out of my dream. 'Oh, Ricky,' she said, 'I don't know how many times I'm going to ask you.' Well, of course it was her breath that smelled of peppermint—they kept them on the counter of the tanning clinic.

I swung my legs onto the floor. 'They weren't even on the couch,' I said. 'I don't fit.'

She bent over and kissed the top of my head. 'Tired, sweetie?'

'Nope,' I said. She was always thinking I was tired because of my spurts, as she called them.

Mum went over to the kitchen and put some grocery bags on the bench. 'I've been like a walking zombie all afternoon. Feel like I'm getting something, a cold or something.' She pointed at the top cupboard. 'Would you mind, hon?'

I reached up and put a pack of paper towels in the cupboard. Not that long ago I'd needed a chair, then a stool, then tiptoes. Now it was an easy reach.

I peered inside the bags. 'I'm hungry.'

'All those vegetables are just not doing the trick, are they?'

No mother likes a vegetarian. I looked at her; she was a different colour. 'What happened to your face?'

'Oh, I had a wee session at the end of the day.'

'Is that tanning?'

'It's a pick-me-up.'

The brown was unnatural. She was red around the ears too. 'Sunbeds cause cancer.'

'Not our ones, Ricky. You're talking about UV. We're safe with what we do.'

We'd had this conversation before.

'It's all the same, Mum. You're gonna die if you do that.' She was stacking things in the fridge. I watched a jar of gherkins go in. 'Can I have that?' She handed me the jar.

'The clients have to see us tanned anyway,' she said. 'They don't want to see pasty people, sick-looking pale people, on the front desk.'

'Yeah right,' I said, 'they want to see people with skin cancer. There's stuff in bottles you can use if you want brown.' I drew out three gherkins.

'Oh, no, those solutions, they go everywhere on your clothes, Ricky. We wear white. Now get out of my way while I do dinner, and don't eat the whole jar beforehand.'

I moved to the door. Mum called out to me, 'How'd it go today with your book thing? Do you have basketball practice tonight? Let's eat early so you're not playing on a full stomach.'

I lay on my bed, eating the gherkins. I was looking at my poster of the St Louis Gateway Arch. If you've never seen the arch, you're probably thinking of something wrong. The Gateway Arch is a silver curve, like half an M, reaching six hundred feet into the air and coming back to earth again. It catches the sun and the sky, and that gives it a million moods, caught in a million calendars sold all over the state of Missouri, which is in the Midwest. But I'm not here to throw a bucket of cold water over the experience. It is something to be in the presence of the arch. If you put your hand to the cool metal side, the arch sings through your fingers and up your arm. You feel connected to a power that might just shake you to bits even though nothing is moving except the clouds reflected in the silvery mirror of metal.

We went there. All the way to Missouri. When it was still America. I felt it, that arch. I thought for a moment that I had an arm made of some silvery metal, though it was hardly metal—it was softer than metal but still with its strength and stretching into the sky, curving not over itself at the apex but over the horizon and pitching me over it, too.

I remember what my dad said. He said, with a shrug, 'It's quite good.'

From him that was high praise. Praise for a high thing.

One other thing: my grandfather helped build it, which was why we went there on our US holiday via Disneyland (me) and Indianapolis (Dad) for the car race. The idea was we each chose a destination and had to not only go along with the others' choices but enjoy them—or pretend to. This proved hardest for my dad. He didn't like rides. Strangely, the navy had ruined him for motion-based activities—he even got carsick if he wasn't driving. The most violent thing he went on at Disneyland was the Mad Hatter, where the three of us were waltzed gently around in giant teacups. When he stepped out of the cup, he was green. St Louis was another trial.

As a young man, Mum's father had lived in the States. He'd died when I was a baby. In St Louis he'd worked on one of the creeper derricks—the thing that climbed the legs, adding on the sections. Each section was 12 feet high and weighed 50 tonnes. Ordinary cranes couldn't get up above 72 feet. My grandfather worked on the arch for eight months. He went up to the derrick platform in a passenger elevator every day. They had a toilet up there. One time, apparently, he fell. A stupid slip, he said. But he was wearing a harness. He ended up dangling in mid-air hundreds of feet above the ground.

Mum and I went up inside the arch, before I grew. It was six hundred feet in a strange sort of jerky lift. My dad wouldn't go up. 'Come on, Stevie,' Mum said.

'I can't go,' Dad said, turning away from the ticket place.

At the top, Mum and I peered through a slit of a window out across the river and East St Louis. 'Look,' said a man to his wife—we were sharing the viewing with a group—'you can't even tell that's a city in ruins.' He was American.

'Breaks my heart,' said his wife.

I looked over at my mum and her eyes were glistening. 'Are you all right?' I asked.

She smiled at me, took a tissue from her bag, and wiped her eyes. 'Fine,' she said. 'What I was thinking was your grandfather built this. My dad.'

The man who'd spoken to his wife overhead Mum and said, 'He did a fine job, ma'am.'

'Thank you,' said my mum.

Then the man shook my hand and told me well done, though I'd done nothing. He stamped on the floor. 'You think it'll hold?' he said. His wife hit him gently and told him to stop it. He was grinning at us. 'You know about the thirteen, I suppose?'

'Sorry?' said Mum.

'The thirteen.'

We shook our heads. I could tell Mum wanted to get away from the man. She was already turning around, looking at her watch. The man switched his attention back to me. 'Your grandfather was a lucky man.'

'Yes,' I said.

'In the construction of this arch, they estimated thirteen

workers might lose their lives. But no one did. Amazing for the kind of project it was.' He was smiling at me once more. I didn't like him, either. Why talk about death up here?

'Everyone must have been really careful,' I said.

'That's it,' said the man. 'They must have been real careful.'

'My father was always very safety conscious,' said Mum.

'Had to be,' said the man. 'But why thirteen, you might ask?'

'They didn't ask,' said the man's wife. 'You'll have to excuse my husband. He's obsessive with large structures.'

'Thirteen because of height, maybe. It's sure a long way down. Previous experience, previous deaths. There was a formula worked out for bridges. Goes back to the 1930s. Rule of thumb was to expect one fatality for every one million in cost. Golden Gate Bridge cost thirty-five million but only eleven construction workers died. That was a great record. See, they had nets for the first time. The net saved nineteen guys. If you fell into the net, you became a member of the Halfway to Hell club. Halfway down, you think is this it? Is that net going to work? Or. Yeah. What a thing. I don't know about the arch, though, how exactly they figured thirteen. Nets were just one improvement. Other improvements came along. Still, it was dangerous. Construction is dangerous, period.'

I was about to tell the man about my grandfather's slip and how the harness had saved him. But I didn't.

'Well,' said Mum, 'they were brave souls who made it for us to come up.'

'Sure,' said the man. 'Next time they would have guessed less fatalities, I suppose. You folks aren't from round here. I detect an accent. Australia!'

When we got down, I said to Dad, 'Why didn't you come?'

'I have an ear thing, an infection. I can't be up high.'

'Is it your back?'

'What back?'

'I thought it might have been your back was sore.' Periodically he had back issues from all that bending over engines. It was unspoken that we never speak about his problems with motion sickness.

'What are you talking about? I said an ear infection. Anyway, you look across the river, I suppose. What was it like?'

'It was beautiful,' said Mum. 'Gateway to the West.'

That was what my poster said. Gateway to the West.

Whenever I heard the word gateway, saw it written, I had a strange feeling. A shiver went through me. Wasn't I looking for a gateway? To what?

But high up in St Louis, looking down, there was no gateway, only a general flatness. Did America ever end? To be honest, I'd liked the arch from the ground better, just touching it. The man had ruined it somehow.

'Always remember,' said my mother, 'your grandfather helped build that.'

'He never let me forget it,' said my dad.

'He was proud,' she said. She walked off ahead of us.

'Oh, boy,' Dad said to me. 'If any of us leave this world without completing a six-hundred-foot public monument, our lives have been failures.'

Somehow I couldn't think of my grandfather now without thinking of the man up inside the arch, telling me about the thirteen workers. I started telling my dad about this, but there was a woman carrying a child and trying to get her baby buggy up some steps and Dad went off to help.

In the evening of the arch trip, we went to the stadium and saw our first and only professional baseball game. The stadium was a huge sparkling circle with three levels of seats. We sat in the uppermost level. I remember thinking how many people were expected to die in the construction of this stadium. And did they? And who'd ended up in the Halfway to Hell club?

The local team, the Cardinals, lost badly to the Pirates of Pittsburgh. The man beside us was getting furious as the game went on.

'Goddam Pirates,' said the man. 'What a day.'

'It's just a game, Dougie,' said the woman beside him.

'Oh, please,' said the man called Dougie. 'I'm a better shortstop.'

We watched another Pirates batter hit a home run into the night sky. Dougie glanced at me and crushed his beer cup in his hand. 'Do they know there are children watching?' he said. Then he said to me, 'You play ball?'

I wondered, Americans are always talking.

Dad said, 'He plays softball. We're from New Zealand.'

'New Zealand!' The man shook his head. 'Well I need to apologise on behalf of my city and my state that you've come all that way to witness this.'

Mum leaned forward, smiling, and said, 'We're loving our time here!' Then she was talking about the arch.

In the stadium shop Dad bought me a Cardinals cap with the red bird on it, and I wore it playing softball.

Before I grew, softball was the thing.

I liked to be the catcher.

That's because you always want to be involved in the game, my dad used to tell me.

Hmm, I'd say.

I was like you, he said.

Hmm.

Because you want to be in there, not loafing around or picking daisies or doing handstands like some kids.

One time Dad came to a softball game and Ben Dreaver was patrolling the outfield upside down. When the ball came near, Ben walked towards it on his hands. People were shouting at him but he took his time.

You're not some dreamer, my dad would say.

Some Dreaver, you mean, I said.

What?

Never mind.

When my dad was in the navy, he got a tattoo. It ran down his left bicep and said *Gimme a break*. This was way before he had a family. He'd grown up in Auckland. Became a mechanic, joined up on a whim. Devonport Naval Base. Sailed the world. I never saw the world, he'd tell everyone. Too bloody busy keeping the ships running.

All of that part of his life I couldn't understand. He went to sea? Naval guns were fired? He played softball? He was a boy?

One night I was lying in bed, and I thought if I'd been the same age as my father, would I have been his friend? Or avoided him? Would he have hated a boy like me? The only way I could get to sleep that night was to construct an elaborate story of how we—my father and I—both the same age, started off as enemies and then somehow ended up best buds. But how did we do it? I couldn't remember when I woke up.

Was he right about softball and me?

Behind the batter, it was true, you were involved in every ball. You called the play. You watched the runners. You were coiled, ready to throw, to tag. But that isn't why I liked it. I liked it because ... you could stop the game. The play ended each time the ball entered your glove. For a moment you had decided, through the act of catching, that this particular segment was finished. Until you threw the ball back, the world was still. It was waiting. Nothing more can happen. It was all yours.

In three weeks it would be the 30th of October. Oh, Mike, Mikey. I could feel it coming. Same date as the Aspiring fair and our human library. Spring had sprung, everyone said. Look at the blossoms! Along the lakefront, across the road, the trees that took the brunt of the wind and had grown away from the water were a flaming mix of pink and white flowers. Campervans were stopping in places they shouldn't so people could take photos. It made my dad mad. Have they never seen a tree? What caves have they emerged from that a bit of colour causes them to lose their minds? But the trees were pretty, and the blossoms that fell on our car—it seemed a shame to wipe them off.

4.

If you're tall, people always ask about basketball, they don't ask about softball. I didn't care much about the hoopy game, though as a favour to my school I played, and because my friends Sim and Johnny, both good, experienced players, said I'd be a fool not to.

They had a point.

When they saw me, opposition teams lost their game plan. They kind of panicked and tried to keep the ball away from me, so they ended up going against our best players. I was not among those best players. 'Thing is, Ricky,' Coach Dennett told me, 'you don't even have to know the rules, you're worth ten, fifteen points.' I knew the rules but there were shorter guys—much shorter—who had real passion and skill. All they lacked was height. I was awkward on court but guys bounced off my shoulders, and when the ball came I usually caught it and handed it on in the appropriate direction. In this fashion we had progressed to a play-off game. Win there and we were off to the regionals; beyond that, the nationals. More than a few people—fair enough—were quite excited about all of this.

'When you fill out,' Dad had told me, 'you're going to be a very imposing figure on the horizon.'

Mum, aside from reminding me not to loom and asking if I was tired, never liked any mention of my height. 'Don't go giving him a complex,' she said.

Actually, I was quiet a lot, feeling like I didn't want to speak. I was disappearing to the upstairs brain room, a second floor added on, and that's where I went and looked out on the world through a narrow slit.

I stood now in the living room, looking at the TV—even the TV had become smaller; I had a different view of it, peering down. I saw the dust on it. It wasn't that I was unhappy. I was thinking. Often they can look like the same thing.

My mum glanced up at me and said, 'What's going on up there?'

'Nothing,' I said. In my jeans pocket, my fingers curled around the fifty-dollar note Mr Le Clair had given me.

'You look a bit … I don't know. Everything's okay, isn't it, Ricky?'

'Sure.'

'Anxiety,' she said.

'What?' I said.

'There's a lot of anxiety issues among young people. There was a thing about it on the radio when I was driving home.'

'I'm okay.' Oh, sure. I was a walking freak show. When people saw me, they took out their tape measures, like I was a prize vegetable grown for some competition. I could have told her then, I suppose, about Le Clair and Garth, the betting in the back room. The car, the nose. But she would have told me I had to quit the job. Why would this man give you fifty dollars? Who was he? She wouldn't have liked it.

'If ever you want to talk, Ricky.'

'Mum, I don't need to talk.'

'Not to me, obviously.'

'I'm fine.'

'Okay,' she said.

I went upstairs to get my jacket and I ended up taking my brother Mike's softball glove out of the drawer. Then I put the glove over my face. Inside the glove I could wear my true face. I was me. Or I was a nothing that didn't have to be a something. I must have looked weird.

I thought when my dad puts his head inside the engine of his Camaro, is he really himself? His weird self?

And my mum? Did she have a glove, too, where she could go? When she was frying under the lamp at her work, eyes closed behind sunglasses, was she also going, ahhh?

On my way to basketball practice, I was stopped on the street by a couple of older kids, maybe seventeen or so. One was 5'9" with sneakers, the other was a little shorter. The shorter one had leather boots with silver straps. They wanted me to buy beer for them from the bottle store across the road. There was two bucks in it for me.

I said no, I didn't want to get in trouble. Anyway, I told them, I'd never bought alcohol before. I was just a kid.

'Pull down your cap,' said the guy in the boots. 'Go to the cooler, get two six-packs of DB. Put them on the counter with the twenty bucks on top. The guy'll be sorting out your change before he's even seen who it is.' I said if it was that easy why didn't they do it. 'We don't have your advantage, man,' said the other one.

That word 'advantage'—it was the same word Mr Le Clair had used. It struck me now that Le Clair had also predicted this scenario, or something like it. He'd said it would be my buddies asking. These weren't my buddies.

They were already pressing the twenty-dollar note into my hand. This was my new life—money coming my way for all sorts of new and dodgy activities. Perks.

One of them took out his phone. They posed beside me for a selfie.

'The guy knows my old man,' I said.

'It's not the guy, he's on holiday. It's someone new.'

They were right. The dude in the store didn't even look at my face—looking up was an effort he wasn't prepared to make. Plus he was Spanish or Italian or something—most of Aspiring's service staff were young travellers holed up for the skiing or the windsurfing or the tramping or whatever. He gazed somewhere into my chest and gave me credit for the two-plus years I didn't have. My heart was banging. I scooped the change off the counter and left with the beer.

Outside the store I felt suddenly strange. A year ago, I'd been 5'5", buying chippies. Guys like the ones whose beer I was now carrying would have pushed me off the pavement, if they'd paid me any attention. It was only a foot difference but my former life seemed to exist on another world far, far away and to which I would never return.

'You want a drink?' said the one in sneakers.

My dad had given me sips from his beer when he was in a good mood, watching the rugby. Beer, I guessed, was something you grew into. I wondered how long it would be before I was buying beer for myself and my friends. I was definitely going to be the one. There was no one among my friends who had a chance.

'No, thanks,' I said. 'My folks'd smell it on me, you know.'

They were so happy and excited to have their beer they didn't listen to my reply. I began to walk off. 'Hey,' said the one with the boots, 'you're a regular lighthouse, man! Warn the boats where the fucking rocks are!' The two of them were still laughing as I turned the corner. *He was scarcely aware of making an effort such was the strange power in his long arms as he reached out, grabbed their necks, and brought the heads of the two boys together with a loud crack.*

I cut through the back of the school and came across Johnny, our point guard, outside the gym, smoking a cigarette. He heard my steps and quickly threw the cigarette away into some bushes.

'Oh, man, you scared me, Ricky,' said Johnny. He looked over towards the bushes. 'That was a waste of half a smoke.' He'd got the cigarettes cheap from an older cousin who lived in Christchurch who said he'd got them from a bloke in a pub. Johnny said that when he was done with his secret stash—thirty packs—he'd quit forever.

'Is Coach Dennett here yet?' I said. 'Aren't we late?'

Johnny shrugged. 'You grow some more today?'

'Maybe,' I said.

'I think you did, Clemens. I think you're taller today. It's not fair.'

'Stockton was only five-nine,' I said. Our Johnny, who idolised NBA legend John Stockton, was 5'7" but hadn't grown in months.

'Stockton was a genius, Ricky. I shouldn't even be saying his name aloud.' He watched Stockton videos on YouTube most days and tried to copy his moves.

'Give up the smokes then.'

Johnny looked again towards the bushes where he'd thrown his cigarette. 'Clemens, if you were my height and static with a dream of playing pro ball, you'd be smoking, too. It's called nerves. It's called despair.'

We walked into the gym and Coach Dennett yelled from the far end, where the other guys were doing sprints, 'The long and the short of it!'

'Kiss me, you mean old mother,' whispered Johnny.

'Good of you to show up, guys,' said Coach Dennett. He strode over to us. 'Now get down and give me twenty.'

Johnny groaned and Coach Dennett put a hand on his head. 'You shrinking or something, Tyler?'

'No, Coach,' said Johnny.

Coach turned to me. 'You think he's getting smaller, Clemens?'

'No, Coach,' I said.

'Then what's up?'

Sim, one of our forwards and our friend, called out, 'I think Clemens just grew again, Coach.'

All the guys started laughing except Johnny, who looked pissed off.

'You grow again, Clemens?' said Coach Dennett.

'Don't know, Coach,' I said.

'My God if you could actually play this game,' said Coach Dennett, 'we wouldn't be able to move in this place for scouts. Steven Adams watch out. You know that, don't you, Clemens?'

'Yes, Coach.'

'You know you're squandering one of the most remarkable growth spurts in the history of adolescence, don't you, Clemens?'

'Yes, Coach. Squandering it, Coach.'

'There's kids here who'd kill you to get your inches.'

'Kill me, yes, Coach. If they could find the secret.'

'You all right, Clemens?'

'Yes, Coach.'

'Hey, Tyler,' said Coach, 'you think you'd kill Clemens for his inches if you could have them?'

'I'm a point guard,' said Johnny. 'I only need another two. Stockton was only—'

Coach Dennett cut him off. 'John Stockton was a bona fide

41

genius, Tyler. Not only was he that but he was the exception to the rule. Clemens is the rule and Stockton was the exception. To be the exception you must be a genius. Are you a genius, Tyler?'

'No, Coach.'

'I think you're some guy who can pass a ball okay and dribble through his legs and lay off something for some other guy. Am I being unfair? You're a guy with a brain for the game, which actually puts you above Clemens here. You can read a game okay, all that, but you're also a guy who can't be bothered getting to the gym on time. Everyone else manages. Hell, some of your team-mates arrive early! I found Angus waiting for me to open up.'

Someone called out, 'Angus has a new spring in his step, Coach.'

There were giggles.

'I think he has,' said Coach Dennett. 'I think Angus is a role model.'

A cheer went up.

'With the regionals in our grasp, I think Angus's attitude shows us the way. In our grasp, boys!' Coach Dennett raised an arm, pumping the air, and the rest of the boys went 'Ooo! Ooo! Ooo! Regionals!'—it was our team chant. He turned back to Johnny. 'And I hope to heck that isn't nicotine I can smell.'

'Coach?' I said. 'Do you mind if I sit out for a bit? I just had a big dinner.'

Coach Dennett threw his arms in the air. 'Why do I bother? Why do I?'

After practice I walked with Johnny and Sim back into town. We always hung out together. Johnny was chewing gum to clear his breath of cigarettes. We were wheeling our bikes. People say it's fun to ride bikes with your friends but I preferred this: wheeling them, just dawdling, hoping never to get home. It was dark but still light under that wide sky, with a weird illumination coming from the mountains. A cat crept under the wheels of a parked car outside the pharmacy and watched us go by. You didn't see many cats in Aspiring. Dogs were alpine. Cats were sea level. A cat in the snow was a goner. A dog in the snow was just having fun. A cat would run from a lake.

The cat studied us carefully, disdainfully. The cat made me think of Mr Le Clair. Was it the long thin nose? The overall darkness? The creeping, the hiding and the showing? Gone one moment, here the next.

What if Le Clair was involved in something?

'Do you think,' I said, 'that there's organised crime operating in Central Otago?'

'Gangs you mean?' said Sim. 'P?'

'Too cold for gangs down here,' said Johnny.

'They got their leather jackets and stuff,' said Sim.

'I've never seen a brown dude park his Harley outside Base 2.'

'Not necessarily P or anything,' I said. 'Or the Mongrel Mob.'

'Who then?' said Johnny.

'I don't know. Other … mobs. Just crims, working together.'

We paused while Johnny adjusted his bike seat.

'Why anyway, bro?' said Sim.

'Nah, never mind,' I said.

Johnny said, 'No reason our little town would be exempt from the illegalities and depravities of the wider universe. So sure. Why not. Connected guys walk among us, yeah.'

'Listen to this guy!' said Sim.

Johnny shrugged.

We walked along in silence for a while until we got near Sim's house, then I said, 'So, Johnny, these connected guys are like everywhere, huh?'

'Course they are,' said Johnny. 'They're into anything that moves.'

'What specifically in Aspiring?'

'There's a shitload of building going on,' Johnny said. 'The new subdivisions. Contractors everywhere. That's money, isn't it.'

We thought about that for a moment.

'Queenstown maybe,' said Sim. 'But the action in Aspiring? We don't even have a proper airport. We don't have a proper hotel. Where would these guys even stay?'

'Airbnb,' said Johnny.

'Right!' said Sim. 'Here to put the squeeze on the Paper Plus.'

'There's money in everything,' I said.

'No,' laughed Sim, 'I got it, I got it—to put the squeeze on Ricky's dad's garage!'

I laughed at that, too. 'Anything that moves,' I said.

'Look around, bro,' said Sim. He was older than us; he was already sixteen. 'Shush up and look around and listen. Sure this town is expanding but take a listen. The chippies are all dozing in front of the TV. Same as the sparkies, the plumbers. The guys who drive the diggers, they're buggered. They've fallen asleep with their cups of cocoa in their laps. We don't do crime here. We live in a bubble. Remember the sheep rustling last year? That's our kind of crime. Coaxing a mob of sheep into the back of a truck. That's our mob! Where is our graffiti even? Where are the hoodlums? *We* are the fucking hoodlums! The hoodlums are too busy snowboarding, man. The hoodlums are too busy trying to qualify for the fucking X Games!' He waved an arm. 'Listen.'

We stood motionless, listening. We listened to Aspiring in

the evening. We listened and listened to the houses around us, to the trees softly shedding their blossoms, to the lost cats fixed in behind car wheels, to the power lines and the phone wires and the stars above us. To the ice moving on the mountain tops. To the silent lake. We listened to our own breathing. We listened to our own lives. Sim was right. There was nothing moving. All was quiet, all was still. Gangsters had no business in Aspiring. There was not a blade moving in the grass. Not a bug on any blade.

'See you losers later,' said Sim.

Johnny leaned across and tried to kiss Sim on the cheek. Sim shoved him off. 'The hell are you doing, Tyler?' said Sim.

'That's what they do,' said Johnny. 'In the mafia. If you're family, you get a kiss on the cheek from the men.'

'Another good reason it'd never take off here,' I said.

Johnny and I wheeled our bikes for another few minutes. He was talking about the play-off game. I was half listening. Finally he got on his bike and said he needed to burn off his nerves.

'What nerves?' I said.

'Whenever I start thinking about the game, I get wound up. Wish I was laid-back like you.'

I thought about it for a second. 'I'm not laid-back.'

But he'd pushed off ahead into the night.

I looked across the street. I was directly opposite my Aunt Rena's house. She never pulled her curtains. *If people want a show, I can give them a show.* But there were no lights on. When my brother Mikey died, Rena came to stay at our house. She was living overseas then and dropped everything to come to Aspiring. I didn't really remember it. She ended up staying for several months until apparently she fell out with Dad. It was a thing between Mum and Dad, the long-ago business with Rena. Then last year she came to live in Aspiring. Her man had a job here.

Then her man didn't and he left. Goodbye! But Rena stayed. She taught piano in her front room. Any time you want to escape, Ricky, she told me, you have a place here.

Escape what? I wondered.

5.

There was another 30th of October, the first one if you like. I should tell you now.

Once upon a time, as you know, I had an older brother. I don't remember it. I was five years old and Mike was ten. What happened: the car Mike was travelling in to Dunedin blew a tyre and went down a bank. Mike was going to a softball tournament with his best friend, Hamish Saker, and Mr Saker was driving. The Sakers weren't badly hurt but Mike's neck was broken, clean, they said clean, I remember that. He was killed straight off and it was 'peaceful' everyone said, or as peaceful as hurtling down a bank and being thrown around like a doll can be, and it was a clean break.

Gimme a break.

My dad, whose business was and is cars, went around saying, No one blows a tyre unless it's on an eighteen-wheeler and even then you've got seventeen wheels left. A puncture is a slow thing. The air leaks. You end up slowing down. How did the tyre on that vehicle give out? How did that happen on that corner of that road?

He'd been saying it for years before I heard him say it. He'd not serviced the Sakers' car or had anything to do with the tyres on it but he took this, well, personally. I should have taken a look at those tyres, he said. Why didn't I just take a quick look? Before they set off. When they came to pick up Mikey, I could have just quickly bent down, no trouble, and given them the once over. I can gauge tread from yards away. But did I look? No, I didn't. I just waved them off. Bye! Play well! Do your best, boys! And my mum would say, Stevie, spare yourself and us. For whatever terrible reason, the tyre failed at that moment. Please stop talking about the tyre, I'll go mad. I was there, too. I waved them off. I kissed our son goodbye. Remember it was already dark. Remember you are not in the habit of checking the tyres on the cars of our friends. I was there, too. Now please no more. I'll go crazy.

They had running arguments that are easy for me to summon. The words have worn grooves in my head.

Here comes the bit about the tyre.

Here comes the bit about Rena. How long she stayed.

But now I'm trying hard to summon my brother. Those grooves aren't so deep. What was he like? Sure there are photos, but if you were to ask me about the sound of his voice or anything, I'd find it difficult to be accurate.

I remember there used to be someone else in the bedroom with me at night. A body, sleeping and breathing. This presence in the room at night was Mikey. And now there was just a bed. I listened hard to the empty bed. Sometimes it creaked.

Then, after two years or more, my folks shifted the bed out of the room. I remember saying, But what if I want a friend to sleep over? My mum said, Then you can sleep in the lounge or on the lawn in the little tent for an adventure. It turned out that one time I'd been sleepwalking and ended up in Mike's bed. When Mum looked into the bedroom that morning, she got a huge fright, seeing a boy sleeping in Mike's bed. That was why they got rid of the bed.

In the Sakers' car, Mike had been wearing the softball glove. He liked to wear the glove to and from games apparently. Or any time. It was taken off him at school a few times when he wore it in class. He wore it to the movies. He tried a few times to bring it to the dinner table, hiding his hand under the table, eating with the other hand. Sometimes Mum would say, Mikey, are you wearing that glove again? But he wasn't. It was just that his hand smelled of the glove. When he grew up he was going to play softball for New Zealand. Third base, because he had a powerful arm and could throw it fast to first.

Bury the glove, my dad said. I don't wanna see it.

No, my mum said. I'll die if we bury the glove.

That's Mikey's glove, said my dad. Belongs with him.

I'll jump in the hole with him, may as well, said Mum.

The reason I know they said these things is that they repeated them. They spoke in their bedroom, where they thought I couldn't hear them, and mostly I couldn't. But I heard enough. It was their anniversary argument. Every 30th of October. What to do, what should have been done, with the glove. First it was the tyre and then it was the glove. They needed these objects. They'd already got rid of the dog.

My dad would yell, I'm going to get that glove right now and throw it in the rubbish!

Somehow Mike's softball glove had ended up in the glass cabinet in the lounge. My dad never looked in the cabinet. He avoided it. It was like the lake. What lake? When he had to get something

49

out of the cabinet—a bowl or the fancy wine glasses—he sent me. He passed the cabinet with his head turned.

One day—I must have been eight or nine—I took it from there and went and played ball with my friends. Sim and Johnny, others. I showed my friends my brother's name written in the glove. That's my brother, I said. But he's dead.

They were all amazed and I felt wonderful to have a dead brother and to have his glove with his name written inside it in his own handwriting. I said, He was wearing this glove when he died.

Is there blood? they asked.

No, I said, he broke his neck and it was a clean break.

Can we touch it?

No. But you can look.

Why can't we touch it?

This is what he had on him, what he was wearing when he died, I told them. You may as well ask to touch his body.

But you're allowed, they said reverently.

Yes, I said. He was my brother. He was going to play for New Zealand.

When I got home Mum caught me with the glove and suddenly I was saying all this stuff about missing Mike and wanting to be near something that had been his and why was the glove in the glass cabinet where it couldn't be touched and wasn't it better to let Mike's glove have a life.

When I started in on the speech, I was just making it up. But by the time I'd finished, I was crying, and my mum went quiet and finally she said she would talk to my dad about it.

Outcome: I could use the glove. I heard them upstairs arguing. I don't care about the glove, said my dad. Give it to him! Maybe he'll lose it somewhere and we'll be done with it.

Here's the strangest thing though. Once I had it, and had

been given permission to use it, I didn't want to. I kept it in my drawer and I only took it out when I was alone in my bedroom, and only then once in a while. I had my catcher's glove anyway by then. Next I was growing. Next I was leaving planet Mikey.

We used to celebrate the anniversary of the accident. The Sakers would come round for a piece of cake. Just like old Mrs Milton and her grown-up daughter from the fire. The photos would get pulled out and someone would remember some little funny thing Mikey had done. He had this saying. He had this funny way of … Hamish Saker would look at the carpet. But also he'd look quickly at the glass cabinet. Then back to the carpet. My mum would ask about school, what class was Hamish in now and what subjects did he like. Look at you! He would blush, ashamed of growing up, of getting older. And my dad would say to me, Take Hamish outside and do something. We'd go into the back garden and, without talking, slowly pass the rugby ball back and forth until it was time for the Sakers to go home. You have it—pass—no, you have it—pass. No you have the damn ball. I don't want it.

Then the Sakers couldn't make it one year and it was kind of a relief because the next year they didn't come either, but still the three of us would sit round with the cake and the photos, trying to remember the little things Mike had done. Finally there wasn't a cake, just a prayer for Mike from Mum, who usually didn't say prayers, or not aloud and not visibly. At the dinner table when she started speaking and clasping her hands, my dad and I knew enough to bow our heads, and when she'd finished, my dad said Amen, a word I'd only ever heard him use as part of the phrase 'amen to that'.

Gloves. Now I come to think of it, my mum had a glove. But it was for golf. I didn't understand it. Just one glove. On the left hand for a right-handed player. Why not two? There was no ball to catch. You handled a golf ball like an egg. Until you hit it of course, which you did with all your might. You cracked that egg. Mum was a good player, a regular mid-weeker with the ladies on a thirteen handicap. Much, much better than my dad, who played only occasionally and who flew at the ball with ill-temper or tried to steer it carefully—both approaches a disaster. The golf glove my mum wore wasn't protective, not a tough shell but soft, like a second skin, like something beneath a shell, now revealed.

Dad couldn't stand golf gloves. If he found a glove lying around the house, he lifted it on the end of a screwdriver, carrying it to Mum in this way. You dropped something, I believe. As if it were a sock, a dirty handkerchief.

He'd discovered that the golf gloves on sale at all Trump courses were made from the skins of small animals bred for the purpose. The skins were stretched over the hands of carefully selected corpses with rigor mortis. A selection of male corpses and female corpses ensured they were able to supply discerning players with the right size for their games. Small sizes were a special focus. If he could find the evidence for this, it would end the presidency. Or not.

Ugh, where was the off button for my mind? My thoughts jumped from branch to branch like demented birds.

Oh, and this: the difference in temperature between the ice age and our age? Just 5 degrees Celsius. We learned that in science. I watched the lake, thinking, *You* know. We are fools but you know everything.

6.

Saturday. My mum no longer minded me sleeping in since I was obviously 'recovering' from what my body was doing to me. I was the victim in this scenario. For her it was as though someone—or two people—had me by the feet and by the ears and were pulling as hard as they could. Under this sort of pressure there was little wonder I needed to stay in bed all morning. Ahead of the play-off game for the regionals, she also believed I should be cotton- balled. She'd heard this word from someone at the tanning clinic. It didn't stop her doing the vacuuming or banging around in the kitchen. And my dad certainly didn't subscribe to the picture of his son on the rack. Or cotton-balling.

There was noise, let's say. And it was hard to stay asleep. Plus these little waking dreams I wanted to shake: a cat wrapping its tail around my legs. I look down. The cat has Mr Le Clair's face. Overall I preferred the talking dog.

Hunger too.

I had half a Snickers bar in my bag, so that kept me going for a while. Ricko Snicko. I tried reading. I tried reading the Snickers wrapper. Then I gave in at midday. We are slaves to our wants and needs, aren't we? We are puny—even if we are tall. I looked up at the arch shining on my poster. On the day the two sides finally met, they trained the hoses of fire engines on the metal to keep it from expanding. A lot of people doubted the two sides would ever meet. The giant thing would be an expensive joke. How could it work when there was one-sixteenth of an inch in it? St Louis would be a laughing stock. People watched it expecting an almighty fail. They thought this foreigner with a funny name, we knew he'd stuff it up. That was Eero Saarinen—he was the designer, the dreamer. Finnish. When they held a competition for a monument, Eero and his father both entered. His father was a famous architect, while Eero was just making his way. They both had the same initials, E. Saarinen, and when the envelope arrived, the father opened it. Yes, he had won the competition in St Louis. There was a bottle of champagne. Well done, Father! Then a telegram came. A mistake had been made. It was the other E. Saarinen—the son's design would stand as the Gateway to the West.

When I told Dad this story, he made a grunting noise and said, 'Why'd they have the same initials? Asking for trouble.'

I went down for breakfast. My dad was at the kitchen table, eating his lunch, looking at a car magazine.

'We don't have any power,' I said into my bowl of Weet-Bix and canned peaches, protein powder sprinkled on top. We'd got this tip from Coach Dennett.

Dad looked up at the lights, then at the light switches. He went back to his magazine.

I hadn't meant to speak aloud—it was only a thought. This gave me a fright. But my dad was one of the great ignorers, capable of ignoring even the things said purposefully. The things my mum said, for instance.

I tried an experiment. 'Strange men are betting on my height.'

'Uh-huh,' said Dad, turning a page. He was shovelling in some eggs. The eggs looked good—scrambled, like I like them. Oh, if only he were to die, I thought, or leave the table at least, I could have those eggs in a second. All it would take to make things good between us was for him to push his chair back and say, 'Here, son, you have these. You need them more than I do.' Weren't we like the Saarinens? The father-and-son team, architects both, who'd come to that moment when the one on the way up passes the one on the way down? Dad thought the eggs were for him but really they had his son's name written on them.

I said: 'A great event is approaching.'

Nothing emerged from him.

I said: 'There's someone who wants me for a mission.'

Zero.

I said: 'Maybe they're up to no good.'

Finally my dad looked up. 'Someone ate all the pastrami last night after I'd gone to bed,' he said. 'Some so-called vegetarian.'

'I thought that was everybody's.' In moments of extreme weakness, I created categories of meat that weren't meat owing to the brilliant disguise of a name. Wasn't pastrami really some kind of thin reddish Italian cheese?

'It was,' he said. 'So, Mr Vego, how come you ate it all?'

'Backsliding after basketball.' I was weak against my own cells, the forces tearing me apart internally. 'I need my strength for the play-off game.'

My dad didn't really understand basketball. In this he was like me. He believed I should have stuck with softball. He suspected, quite rightly, I had very little skill at this strange jumping and dunking thing, except the obvious one of reach.

'How's the team shaping up?' The question was routine, lifeless.

'Good,' I said.

'Good,' he said. He stood up and carried his plate to the bench. 'What are you doing today, Richard Clemens? Coach will have you on some training regime, I suppose.'

'Not really,' I said. 'I'm going into town.'

He rinsed his plate. One time he'd found me licking the plates. There was food on them. I needed to feed the machine. 'Don't do anything stupid, okay?' he told me.

Why did people think I was always going to do something stupid? Did I suddenly seem more stupid? Were overly tall boys more stupid looking than their shorter peers? Probably. It was in our lope. It was in our loose limbs. Our droop.

My dad walked out to the back porch and I saw him pulling on his overalls. He had an old Chevrolet Camaro he was working on in the garage. A 1970 genuine split-bumper RS in original Mulsanne blue. Over the past five years he'd rebuilt it: new engine (small-block 4-bolt main 350ci V8), new transmission (TH 350 automatic), new seats (black vinyl). It wasn't ready for the road yet, though when he started the engine, the glass in our back door shook.

Two years ago or even last year, I had spent a lot of time with Dad and that car. But somehow I wasn't that interested any more. Suddenly it was just another thing I used to do.

Dad spoke to the Camaro sometimes—I'd heard him. Murmured nothings, little admonishments, sweet things. Once or twice he swore. Probably he didn't even know he was speaking aloud, either.

If there was an argument in the house, it usually detoured to the car and the loving he put in there. My mum told him one time that she wanted to be treated as well as the car got treated. She wanted those little murmurs for herself. Another time—a better one obviously—early one morning, I had to get up to go to the toilet and I heard them through their bedroom door, giggling and shushing each other. I stopped and listened. 'Your engine appears to be in excellent working order, madam,' said my dad. Then my mum's voice, 'Did you look under the bonnet? There's something been making a funny noise. Can you check?' 'Let me look again,' said my dad. Muffled, his voice said something else I couldn't catch that made my mum laugh.

Lesson: do not pause and listen in a quiet house. The quiet is never complete, the sounds will draw you in ...

I went out to the garage. Dad was sitting in the Camaro, fiddling with the ignition. Wires lay all over his lap. 'Dad, have you seen a Cadillac round town?'

'What colour?' he said. Cars always got his attention.

'Black.'

'What year?'

'I don't know.'

'What condition?'

'Newish.'

'Newish black Caddy?'

'Yes,' I said. 'But not a long one. A short one.'

'A short one? What do you mean?'

'You'd know it if you saw it. Like it's been cut down. Front and back.'

'Sounds hideous,' said my dad. 'What idiot would want to cut down a Caddy? Can't be a Cadillac.'

'Okay,' I said. I was backing out of there.

'What?' said Dad. 'What's with this car, Ricky?'

'Nothing.'

'Come here and hold this for me,' he said.

I leaned inside the car and took a pair of wires he was holding out to me.

'Now bring them together,' he said.

'Rub them together?' I said.

'Yeah, touch 'em together.'

'No,' I said.

'Why not?'

'Cause they'll spark is why.'

'Good,' said Dad. 'Good boy. Who says you're useless. That's good.'

'*Who says I'm useless*? What kind of self-esteem does that build, Dad?'

'Latest research into self-esteem, Ricky, is that everyone's got too much of it. We all rate ourselves too highly. The problems come when we discover we're not as clever and handsome and charming and multi-talented as we imagined ourselves to be. The more accurate you can get about yourself and your qualities, the better you'll cope with a world that frankly doesn't much care about us. I don't speak to snuff out your dreams and ambitions. We would be nothing without them. Me, I'm hoping to rebuild this heap into something like respectability. It makes sense, though, that you always need to carry in that same wallet of hope the currency of common sense.'

I was backing out of the garage while he spoke. When he'd finished, I said, 'I'm going to meet the guys in town.'

The currency of common sense. While my dad worked on the Camaro, he listened to the radio. He got a lot of stuff off there. He listened to talkback until he'd had enough, then he listened to old music, mostly country. The only music, he said, in which the use of a violin wasn't a criminal offence.

The previous year when Trump was elected, Dad said, 'I'm not surprised one bit.' He went around saying, 'I'm not surprised.'

Everyone was surprised and said so except my dad.

He stuck his head back inside his precious car, singing the lines of a song he liked to sing in my presence. It's called 'Big Boss Man'. I won't quote any lines because you can find it yourself and hum along.

There was a stretch of Saturday that was barren and not easy to contemplate. I was alone, a situation that wouldn't be fixed for a couple of hours yet. I even considered heading to Pete's to see if Garth wanted me for anything.

I Googled world's tallest teenager. 7'8". He was 5'2" in kindergarten. I wasn't so special. I was only the tallest fifteen-year-old in Aspiring. Who knew—maybe Luggate had someone taller, maybe there was some loping goon in Roxburgh who walked the apple orchards, plucking fruit without a ladder. I followed links to Sotos syndrome. Read it and left fast when they got on to life expectancy. But I'd been checked out at Dunedin Hospital. I didn't have a genetic disease. I was 'normal range'. Maybe I should get a t-shirt with that on it. *The girl he'd watched secretly all summer came over to the table, put her fingers out to touch his chest, saying, 'I like your t-shirt.'*

Sim had a weekend job at a shoe store, and Johnny was helping his dad haul up stones from some riverbed out Hāwea way. Johnny's dad ran a landscaping business, dumping dirt and building stone walls and laying brick paths around the new development behind the retirement village. The town was growing and growing. The primary school built a few years ago was already maxed out.

Johnny hated stones, but Coach Dennett had told him to work on his stamina, and Johnny figured that if four hours of heavy lifting were the price for keeping a dream alive, then he would pay it. This didn't mean that he couldn't complain hard and long about brutal exploitation at his father's hands.

We'd arranged to meet by the skate park at three.

I wandered towards town. Passing Rena's house I saw she was in the garden, nursing a cigarette. Why did everyone still smoke? What death wish drove the people in my life? I pretended not to have seen her and ducked my head.

'Hey, Ricky,' she called out. 'Where are you off to?'

'Town,' I said, stopping.

'How's your mum, Ricky?'

I said she was fine.

'She's always such a lovely colour.'

I saw Rena was wearing a dressing gown with dragons up its sides.

She noticed me looking. 'Oh, Ricky, it's too beautiful to get dressed yet, isn't it?'

A long time ago, my aunt sang in nightclubs in Sydney and Brisbane, where they keep different hours. She still lived according to that clock. Rena had never adjusted to what she called civilian life. She and Mum were so different but very close. The closeness was the reason Rena had chosen to remain in Aspiring after her man left. She and Mum met each week for lunch in town. At night if Mum was ever out, it was usually because she'd dropped in to see her sister. Rena would have a glass of wine and Mum would have a cup of tea. Sometimes Mum had wine, too. I could smell it on her breath when she kissed me goodnight. These days the only time she still tried to kiss me goodnight was when she'd had the wine with Rena.

They called each other on an almost-daily basis. Mum would take the calls in their bedroom and I would hear her laughing. Rena hardly ever came to our place.

My aunt was beginning to hum.

'Auntie Rena,' I said, 'would you like to be in a human library?'

She paused her humming. 'What's that, honey?'

'Never mind.'

'How are you, dear Ricky?'

'I'm not anxious,' I said.

'Okay,' she said. 'That's good. Why would you be anxious?'

'I'm not.'

She was smiling at me. 'Ricky, if I ever ask you, "And have you got anyone special in your life?", please shoot me.'

'Okay.'

'But just consider I do have an abiding interest in such things. Okay, sweetie?'

'Okay.'

I said goodbye and turned to leave. A car was going past. It seemed to be slowing. It was the black Cadillac. Soundless as an otter. Snub as a bullet.

The tinted windows made the car seem full rather than empty, as if something was pressed to the glass so tightly no light could enter to make sense of whatever shapes lurked there. When the car was past the house, a shaft of light struck the back window and finally the black tint was punctured. In the back I saw a single head, also like an otter's head, oily wet, freshly combed. Mr Le Clair.

What was he doing here? This was a quiet nothing street, leading nowhere except to respectability. My humming, smoking aunt in her afternoon dragon dressing gown was what? The exception that proved the blah blah blah?

'Friends of yours, Ricky?' my aunt called out.

I shook my head.

'I used to be driven in a car like that,' she said. 'Only longer, I remember.' My aunt had a million stories from her singing days and this wasn't the time for another of them. But the human library could be the time and the place …

As the car turned the corner, I got out my phone and took a picture. My inner voice was silent. As an experiment I said to myself, 'His inner voice was silent', but the sentence ended there. No looping. Le Clair had silenced it. I started to jog towards town, towards the dark ruffled and knowing lake.

7.

At the shoe store Sim was fitting an old guy with slippers. Sim pretended I was a new customer needing immediate attention. He was sole charge after 2 p.m. 'Oh, yes, sir,' he called out to me, leaving the slippers for the old guy to put on by himself. Boxes lay all around. 'It was the trainers, wasn't it?'

At the counter he whispered at me, 'Why are you early? I'm not off for another half hour.'

'I'll hang here,' I said. 'I won't get in your way.'

'Not a good time, Ricky.' Sim checked his watch. He seemed jumpy. 'You really gotta go.'

'Let me get a glass of water from the back.'

The customer was motioning to Sim, waving a slipper in the air. 'Okay, but then you've got to leave.'

'Why? I'll be good.'

'No, no, there's some guys coming in soon.'

'So? You can serve them.'

'You don't get it, bro. You should leave after your water. This is an important job for me and everything, you know.'

'Okay, okay. Who are these guys?'

'No one. Friends of my stepbrother.' Sim was rubbing at the counter with his finger as if there was some stain there he wanted to remove. His stepbrother was a heavy dude.

'What do they want?'

'Don't ask me anything more, Ricky. And don't interfere.'

'In what?'

But Sim had turned back to the old guy with his slippers. I went into the kitchenette out the back to get my water.

Then I heard the buzzer go—twice. The pair had walked in. I looked through the crack in the door. One was short—5'6"—with no neck. He was a human brick in a rugby jersey. The other guy was about Sim's height but bulky. He had on a leather jacket. They were eighteen or nineteen.

The old guy was at the counter, finally sorted with his slippers. He paid and left the store.

Leather said, 'Little Adam, how are you today?' Sim's real name was Adam Simpson. I'd never known him as Adam.

Sim jerked his head in response. I could see he was scared. His mouth opened but no sound came out.

Brick went around behind the counter and stood next to Sim, very close, grinning. 'There should be like three boxes,' said Leather.

Sim bent down, opened a cupboard, and pulled out the boxes. Brick took them from him, saying, 'Thank you, sir.'

'This is the last time, you know,' said Sim. His voice sounded weedy. 'The boss'll find out any day now.'

'Oh, fuck, yeah,' said Leather. 'Last time. Right.'

'Fuck yes, sir,' said Brick. Then Brick brought his foot down on Sim's foot with a stamp and Sim cried out in pain.

That was when I stepped out from the back room. I don't know why I did. Maybe I was surfing on some adrenalin from seeing Mr Le Clair go past my aunt's house. I didn't have a plan. I didn't have my courage screwed up inside me like you sometimes read about.

I'd never been in a fight that wasn't some petty squabble in a playground about whose turn it was. On the basketball court a couple of times, guys had tried to rile me up with elbows and shoves but I'd never taken a swing at anybody. In a couple of years I was probably in line for that title the Gentle Giant. So why was I moving now into the light and heat of this occasion?

It was instinct. It was out of my hands. I took a step and then to maintain balance I took another, like I was on roller skates, moving forward because I hadn't learned yet how to stop and turn. I had no manoeuvres, I only had momentum. It was like I was following myself entering the shoe store, where these two thugs had their little drama going with my friend Sim.

Once arrived I had nothing to say and neither did they—I was a surprise. Everyone just stared and that gave me something like an idea of how to play it. 'What's going on, Sim?' I said.

'Nothing,' said Sim. There were tears in his eyes.

'Who the fuck are you?' said Brick.

'I didn't know it was legal to keep a pet giraffe,' said Leather.

They'd recovered now a little. But I still had a lead on them. Who the fuck was I? They didn't know. Maybe I was crazy and violent.

I said, 'I didn't know it was legal to take merchandise without paying for it.'

'You better move on through now, Mr Giraffe,' said Leather. 'Back in your cage.'

'Yeah,' said Brick.

'I'm just looking out for my friend,' I said.

'You're a look-out all right,' said Leather. 'I thought it was a fucking lighthouse coming outta there!'

Brick laughed at this.

'That's very original of you,' I said.

'I can see right up his nose!' said Brick.

'I can see right onto your bald spot,' I said.

Up to this point, I thought things had gone amazingly well. I was talking, wasn't I? They didn't know what I was capable of. I believed I'd won a kind of respect. What use was this size after all if I didn't use it? I could use it to lean back on the people who were leaning on others. One time my dad said to me that what I had with this height was a new responsibility. I wasn't the same any more, being this size. The size was a gift, he told me, but also a tool and like any tool, you had to learn how to use it. Then suddenly he gripped my arms and said, 'It's so great to see you reach this age.'

'Okay,' I said to my dad.

Then I understood he'd meant Mike—that Mike hadn't had this chance, that my big brother would always be younger than me, smaller, and that his death had made my dad sort of terrified. He was permanently marked by this feeling of dread; it was like his old navy tattoo.

The currency of common sense, I remembered.

But this was common sense.

Sim had been wrong to tell me to keep my nose out of it. He could now see what I could accomplish—I could, too. I was using the tool of my height to help someone. This was what Dad had been telling me about. It was a special moment.

Then Brick punched me.

He swivelled and led with his fist, but behind his fist came that body, that brick, into my stomach. He punched me with his whole brick being.

I went down.

I folded up. I lost everything—my breath, my balance, my height. I was down at Brick's knees, just a fifteen-year-old kid, playing out of his league. One of Brick's knees drew back adjacent to my cheek. He was going to mash my head. His jeans strained everywhere with the wish. I'd thought I was the Hulk, then that Garth was, but here was the real thing.

'Leave him,' said Leather. 'I think he's got the message.'

I closed my eyes on the pain. Then the door buzzer went twice—they were gone.

There was silence for a little bit. Next—crazy thing—a sparrow hopped inside the doorway. He hopped around on the welcome mat, peering and poking like they do. He looked at me and he looked at Sim. What the hell were we doing? He flicked his head from side to side, giving us his eye. We were both looking at the jumpy, stupid, nervous, happy bird.

Quickly the scene grew too strange for the sparrow and he took off with a sound like rubber bands.

'You shouldn't have done that,' said Sim.

I tried to speak but there was only wheezing and struggling.

'What's the matter with you? What were you thinking, to try that? Fuck!' Sim put his hand on my back. 'What an idiot. Didn't I tell you? Didn't I say? How stupid! You've just made things a hundred times worse. I don't know what those guys'll do next. I can't believe you did that. You think you're invincible or something because of those inches you put on? Thing is, Clemens, you're tall but that's all.'

'I hate that song,' I croaked.

'What song?'

'Never mind.'

Sim, with his good foot, kicked at a box of shoes. 'So, anyway,' he said, 'are you all right?'

'No,' I said.

'So they didn't kill us, I suppose.'

Sim sat down beside me on the floor. 'Hey, Ricky, that was incredible what you did, you know.'

'It was so stupid,' I said.

'It was stupid but it was also, you know, brave. True, bro. Trying to help me out and everything.'

'Look what help I brought.'

'Yeah, but it was worth it, man.'

'You think?'

'Probably not. But that was a helluva thing to see.'

'Will they be back?'

'Well I don't think you scared them off if that's what you're hoping.'

'Hey, Sim, what you were saying the other night about Aspiring being this nothing-happens place? Look, it happened. It's happening. We found our hoodlums. We found our organised crime.'

'Those dicks aren't organised. They're from Albert Town.'

When I was ready Sim helped me up. Then he said, 'Ricky, why'd you come in here anyway? What was that about?'

I said, 'Have you seen a black Cadillac round town lately?'

'No.'

I showed him the picture on my phone.

'I don't get it,' he said.

'Nor do I.' I told him about the back-room measuring, the fifty bucks, the collapsed nose.

'What is he, some grooming paedo?'

'Nah, nah, that's not the vibe.'

'What's the vibe?'

'I don't know.'

'Some height-fetish thing.'

I shook my head. It hurt to shake my head. You get punched

in the stomach and it gives you a headache. Interesting. 'Anyway, how's your foot?'

Of course the guy who punched me wasn't the Brick. He was a bowling ball—just as Mr Le Clair had predicted.

8.

We sat under a willow tree—a wallow tree, I call them, all those droopy branches—looking out at the crinkled lake, sipping milkshakes, waiting for Johnny. It was mild, with a light wind at our backs rather than coming into our faces from the mountains. High above us a pair of paragliders circled lazily. Lazily? No doubt there was effort and adrenalin, a touch of fear maybe? Maybe not. I'd never done it, never seen my town while staring down through my dangling feet. But sometimes it felt like that was me … up here. Yoo-hoo.

Sim had been Googling foot injuries. He thought it was broken. I kept my arm over my middle. I thought I had bruised internal organs. It hurt to suck too hard at my shake. We wondered if we could still make the play-off game. For Sim this was a potential disaster and he started to fret. How could we have come all this way to miss out now? It wasn't fair. I told him we'd be okay and he said how could I be sure? If his foot was broken, I said, there was no way he could walk on it. But, Sim said, what if I've broken a toe or something? You couldn't walk on a broken toe, I said. He stared at his foot and said maybe I was right. Then he asked if I thought we'd win the play-off. A play-off for the regionals was unknown territory, I said. Sim said there was more pressure on the opposition than on us because at the start of the season they were expected to win the comp and go through whereas we had already over-achieved. I said that was true. But a lot of people were also talking us up now. They were getting pumped. People like Garth. Sim nodded. Yep, yep. He was getting that, too. Lot of optimism. Fuck optimism, he said. I nodded.

Johnny had texted a while back to say his phone was dying but he'd be here a bit late.

By the boatshed, ducks stood for their photographs in front of the greenish lake. Some tourists obliged.

'Cartoon idea,' I said. 'A group of people around a campfire, toasting their mobile phones on the ends of selfie sticks.'

Sim glanced at me. 'What would the punchline be?'

'I haven't got that far,' I said.

We sometimes played this game. I have an idea for a cartoon. Usually the other person would run with it, come up with a better version of the cartoon—or the words. But Sim had nothing. Neither did I. Maybe this was another thing I used to do.

When Johnny arrived he was already holding up his hands. He was about to tell us about the rocks he'd been carrying to help out his dad. Before he got started, Sim said, 'Shut up, Johnny.'

'What'd I say?' said Johnny.

'We just got beaten up,' said Sim.

'We just took a pummelling,' I said.

'Cool,' said Johnny. 'But what really happened?'

'We got beaten up.'

Johnny sat down on the grass.

Sim cried out, 'Easy on my foot!'

'Boy, you're not kidding, are you.'

Then Sim told Johnny what had happened at the shoe store while I nursed my milkshake.

Johnny listened, occasionally looking at me and then back again at Sim. He was shaking his head and smiling. He couldn't believe any of it—but he knew it was true. When Sim finished, Johnny said he thought we should go to the cops. The police doctor could check us both out, photograph the injuries, and then they could get the guys for assault.

Police doctor? I was pretty sure that apart from New Year's, when they set up containers on the lakefront to act as temporary cells for pissed revellers, Aspiring had a single cop, sometimes joined by a colleague from elsewhere. We didn't have a hospital. There was the medical centre, where most of the rooms were occupied by physios treating adventure sports injuries or working the joints of old people.

Sim told him that was a great idea except for one thing: he wasn't going to the cops. The cops would want to know the whole deal with the shoes and that would lead Sim down a dark path indeed. He'd been supplying his stepbrother's friends with shoes for a couple of months now. That was theft by an employee. He'd lose his job for starters, then he'd be off the team, then he'd be thrown out of school, oh, and then he might be in jail—all of which would be kind of inconvenient to his lifestyle. Next they'd throw his stepbrother in jail.

But Sim was acting under duress, said Johnny. Because they were forcing Sim to do it. That would be part of the charges against them—extortion. 'We were joking about this, weren't we,' said Johnny. 'The mafia and everything.'

'We've done this already,' said Sim. 'This isn't the mafia. This is a pair of arseholes who know my stepbrother. We can't do a thing and we're not going to try.'

'But that means they come back, Sim,' said Johnny. 'They come back every Saturday, and every Saturday they commit a crime. And every Saturday they stamp on your foot and punch someone if they happen to be standing close.'

'Johnny's right,' I said.

'Johnny is not right,' said Sim. 'Anyway, it's my fucking foot and they only did it because I stepped out of line.'

'Stepped out of line!' said Johnny. 'Listen to yourself, Sim. You're taking orders from these creeps now?'

Sim looked at his foot again and moved it around slowly.

'Johnny is right, Sim,' I said. 'It can't go on. But the solution is not the cops.'

'Then what is the solution?' said Johnny.

'I know some people,' I said.

'He knows some people,' said Johnny. 'I don't see you guys for half a day and you've become part of the underworld. Who is it, Ricky?'

'Someone I met at Pete's,' I said.

'The creepy guy who gives you money?' said Sim.

'His name is Le Clair.'

'Who is he?' said Johnny.

'I don't know,' I said.

'What does he do?'

Predicts my fucking future. 'I don't know.'

'Seems to me we got a strong basis for using this guy,' said Johnny. 'What's the deal then, Ricky?'

'He measures me,' I said. 'Bets on my height with Garth.'

'Weird, bro,' said Johnny. 'The more I Iisten to you two, the more I want to go home and help my dad carry rocks.'

We were about to leave but ended up sitting for a bit longer under the wallowing tree because two girls who had walked from their campervan past us, wrapped in towels, now dropped the towels and ran into the cold lake in their bikinis. Maybe they were from Italy or Spain? Portugal or Denmark? *Finland* even? Would they know about their famous countryman who'd made the Gateway Arch? Anyway, they were from the big world, we knew that. They shrieked and gasped, splashed each other, ducked their heads under the water, swam a few strokes, and ran back past us to their campervan, laughing and shaking their wet hair. We got some water sprayed on us. It all lasted in total about two minutes and we watched without speaking. Then we stood up. None of us had girlfriends. Johnny had split up in summer 'to concentrate on basketball'.

Sim gingerly flexed his foot and said, 'Despite all the minuses of today, *that* was an excellent interlude.'

9.

Wednesday evenings at Pete's were slow. I mean Pete's was slow anyway but Wednesdays were glacial. The restaurant was down an alleyway off the main drag, opposite the fourth-most-popular bike hire place in town. You had to be looking—poking your nose around, getting off the beaten track—to make it to our establishment. The flash bars and large chains faced the lake, with everyone else jumbled to the rear in a mess of lanes and odd-shaped carparks. Our front entrance looked out on the back entrances of the fancier places. Our customers fought a maze of wheelie bins and service vehicles. But still, backpackers and randoms seemed to like the search. And we had our regulars who came to sit at the bar. And they liked Wednesdays. These old men who probably weren't old at all, just looked it. The bloke who had a lawnmowing business and who left little grass droppings wherever he sat. Ex-tradies with bad backs who now worked at Mitre 10, stocking shelves. Truckies on their overnight stops. Retired farmers. Occasionally someone would have a black eye or a grazed chin and this was never inquired after. Garth would often come out from the kitchen and sit with them for a while, the unlit ciggie wobbling on his lip. They talked about 'the modern world', as suddenly he was calling it, and the general rottenness of things. Nothing was any good any more, they agreed. Rugby, the weather, the fishing, the music, the cars, the blah blah blah. Aspiring wasn't like it used to be. Grown men skateboarding. Biking. It was all terrible. Shop assistants greeting you in a foreign language. It had gone too far. Where would it end? I'll tell you where, someone would say, Korean Barbecue, that's where. Maybe here someone would say softly, Actually the wife and I tried that the other night and it was quite tasty. But the loud voice, nonsensically, would thunder in: Sometimes I got to remind myself who won that war? It was us, wasn't it?

These men had a great old time together.

And when they shuffled off, Garth said, 'What a bunch of sad losers I waste my time with.'

There was also the odd lost tourist on a Wednesday who, against the wise words of TripAdvisor, had chosen us over the competition. I'd read the comments, the kindest of which said, No nonsense, no frills, no vegetables. Line your stomach here and then get out and enjoy yourself! Another said, Eat at Pete's one night of your Aspiring stay, then you'll really enjoy the other places.

'Where are you from?' Garth would ask.

'From Denver, Colorado.'

'That explains those trousers,' said Garth.

The tourists took Garth for local colour, I guess, and received his insults with happy and nervous grins.

'We are from Ukraine.'

'That explains those haircuts.'

'We are from Belgium.'

'That takes the biscuit.'

'What is this biscuit, please?'

Wednesdays should have been great. Nothing much happening, no pressure on the kitchen, Garth and the broken-down men,

Garth and the grinning puzzled tourists. But they weren't great. For one thing Pete's didn't idle very well. The lack of action pressed down on the place after a while, and it got to the point everyone was just praying some big party would burst through the doors and make a noise and cause some trouble and want to split the bill and everything. Never happened.

Everyone got a little bored and irritable. Garth ended up ordering jobs done that had no meaning beyond inflicting pain and humiliation. Suddenly he wanted the skylight cleaned. Or he wanted the outside bins scrubbed. One time he sent me up into the crawl-space in the roof with a wet rag. I had to lie on my stomach and push myself along with my hands while cleaning. There wasn't room to turn around so when I'd reached the end, I had to back out of the space in the same way. When I came down every muscle in my body had a specific ache and my clothes were covered in grease and grime and Garth called me the human cloth.

Sure, we were waiting for that mythical big rowdy crowd to burst in through the doors, but this waiting was only a cover for our deeper waiting for that sawn-off Cadillac, that chauffeur, that man who put the boss in a sweat.

This Wednesday was no different. I cleaned some pans. I washed down some benches. I swept. I followed Rachel's movements, the way the light caught her white blouse and showed the outline of her bra. If only she would agree to be in my human library—I'd be the first borrower. Nothing sleazy. Her boyfriend was a shearer from Alex. It would just be a chance to stare into her face while she talked about her life.

Instead I listened to Logan talk about his Saturday night (beers at the pub, followed by more beers at home) and Garth, who had this knack, found me doing very little and told me he wondered why he was even paying me.

At that moment Rachel came through and announced we had live customers.

'What do they want?' asked Dave, moving to the griller.

'They want Ricky,' said Rachel.

It was Sim and Johnny. I sat with them in a booth. I had about four minutes until Garth re-emerged ready to chew on the staff again. He pretend-smoked to suppress his appetite but naturally it didn't work.

I asked Sim if he'd had any trouble from his stepbrother. He hadn't as yet because he hadn't seen him.

'Where's the guy?' asked Johnny.

'He's not here,' I said. 'Maybe he won't come. He never calls first. He just shows up.'

'I like that,' said Sim.

'You like that?' said Johnny. 'That he's rude and obnoxious?'

'We might need those qualities,' said Sim.

'Hey, the guy might tell us to go take a flying leap with our little problem of you being intimidated for free shoes,' said Johnny.

'The thing in our favour is he uses me in the betting game,' I said. 'So I think we can ask for something in return.'

'He already pays you,' said Johnny.

This was true. 'I don't know if he'll help or not but it's worth a shot.'

'Remember to do your limp for him, Sim,' said Johnny. 'Underworld crims love a cripple.'

Then the bell went on the door of Pete's, it was opening, and we turned to see who it was. Or rather we turned to see Mr Le Clair—wishing him into existence had worked! I was already seeing the pale hand on the glass door, the pointed boot on the vinyl floor, the dark trouser leg … the door opened … and it wasn't Mr Le Clair at all. It was a girl, about my age. About 5'6".

She looked a bit like someone I knew.

The girl walked past us, raised a hand when Rachel said hello can I help you, and carried on through into the kitchen with Rachel following, saying excuse me but you can't just walk on in there.

'Who is that?' said Sim.

'Don't know,' I said.

'Seems like she owns the place,' said Johnny.

Then it clicked—who the girl looked like. Of course the belly wasn't there, or the greasy skin, or the receding hairline, but something … Maybe in the eyes there was a familiar look, or in the mouth, or in the shoulders—the girl had the beginnings of a swagger. 'That's Garth's daughter,' I said.

'I don't get it,' said Johnny.

'What's her name?' said Sim.

'Keri,' I said. 'I've never seen her before.'

'So where is our guy anyway?' said Johnny.

Sim picked up the sugar shaker and sprinkled some on the back of his hand, then licked it up.

'Don't do that,' said Johnny.

'I need energy,' said Sim.

'You could order some food,' I said.

'I'm broke,' said Sim. He poured some more sugar and Johnny snatched the shaker off him. He stood up with it and said he had to go. His dad was on his case. Sim also had to get moving. It didn't look like Mr Le Clair was going to show anyway.

'Wait another few minutes,' I said.

But I was being summoned. Garth was calling my name from the kitchen. Johnny put the sugar back on the table. 'That's you gone,' he said. 'See you later, Mr Clemens.'

'See you, Mr Stockton,' I said.

'Don't hex me now!' said Johnny.

'Don't hex the little guy,' said Sim, putting his hand on Johnny's head and pushing down as they both went out the door.

Rachel was back at the counter. 'Good luck,' she told me.

In the kitchen Logan handed me a plate of eggs. 'I'm not hungry,' I said.

'Not for you,' said Logan, pointing to the closed door of the office. 'You're just the waiter.'

'What's going on?'

Logan shrugged. 'I'm just the cook.'

I took the eggs and knocked on the door, then I went in. Garth was standing against the far wall with the height chart directly behind him — in this sort of slumped posture, he wasn't more than 5'4". Usually I had the effect of straightening people up, if only temporarily. People wanted to be as tall as they could when they first saw me, but unless they were six feet or more, they tended to rapidly sink back down again — there was too great a difference. You win, they seemed to be saying, we give up. Garth didn't move. He grunted something, which I interpreted as close the door, you idiot.

The girl was sitting behind Garth's desk. She'd looked up briefly when I'd come in and then her head was bent again.

I was still holding the eggs. 'Who wants these?'

No one replied.

I turned to face Garth. He grunted again: Put them down somewhere, I don't care, you idiot. I deposited the plate on the desk; it was almost touching the girl's elbows but she didn't look at the eggs. I reached for the door handle and Garth offered his first full word. 'Stay!'

The word came out with such force and at such volume that the girl was jolted from her position. Suddenly she was taking in her surroundings as if for the first time. She was puzzled by the eggs: how did they get there? She looked at me with the same expression: how did you get here? She seemed to have this reaction to her own body; she looked down at her legs and arms: how'd I get here? Yet she knew enough not to look over into the corner where Garth was standing. She knew all about Garth it seemed. Garth was no mystery.

'This is Ricky,' said Garth to the girl. 'Now eat something.'

'Not hungry,' said the girl.

'Eat anyway,' said Garth.

The girl raised her head again and drew the plate of eggs towards her until it had disappeared. Hunched over, with both elbows supporting her and protecting the plate, she began to eat. There was only the flash of the fork as she shovelled the food into her mouth. She'd finished in no time. Garth watched her; it was like watching an animal that hadn't been fed in a long time and expected the food to be snatched away at any moment. Finally the plate was pushed away and the girl sat a little further back in the chair and wiped her mouth with her hand.

'She's come on the bus from Dunedin. She thinks I should have picked her up from the airport. I was going to pick her up but that was going to be tomorrow. I received incorrect flight information. Plus why didn't she fly into Queenstown? Never mind. We're here now.'

I reached for the plate but Garth told me to leave it. 'Rach!' he shouted through the door.

Rachel arrived quickly and removed the plate. She asked if anything else was required. Garth shook his head and she turned to leave.

'Pancakes,' said the girl.

Rachel looked at the girl and then at Garth. 'Pancakes?' she said.

'She's ordering, isn't she?' said Garth.

'And both of you with such polite manners,' said Rachel, leaving the room.

Garth shifted himself from the wall and sat down on his stool. 'This is Keri,' he said. He was breathing heavily but it was hard to say whether it was heavier than usual. Just standing for a length of time could cause him trouble. 'This is my kid.'

'Hi,' I said.

'He's tall,' said Keri to her father. 'To state the obvious. How tall are you?'

'Six-seven, I don't know,' I said. 'Last time I looked.'

'He's on the chart here,' said Garth, pointing at the wall.

'That was my chart,' she said. 'Back in the day.' She looked at her father. 'Why'd you always want to measure people?'

'To see progress.'

She grunted and glanced at me. 'People probably ask you about basketball.'

I nodded.

She narrowed her eyes. 'I won't.'

'Your mistake then, honey,' said Garth, 'because Ricky is on the high-school team, which is going to the regionals. First time ever for Aspiring!'

'No,' I said, 'we have a play-off first.'

'Yeah, yeah,' said Garth.

Keri looked at me carefully. 'Wow,' she said, flat. 'Are you the tall that can actually, like, *play*?'

'Keri!' said Garth.

I shrugged.

'First time ever the team has done anything!' said Garth.

'We haven't got there yet,' I mumbled.

Again Keri was studying me. She saw that her jibe hadn't

wounded me. 'There are trees that are tall,' she said, 'and you just run around them.'

'Oh, wonderful!' said Garth.

Keri wasn't dumb—she had, okay, my measure—and somehow I liked her. It wasn't clear whether she liked me or not but that didn't seem to matter so much. She was talking. I liked her because she knew what I was and I liked her because she wasn't giving in to Garth. She was also a girl. Was she attractive? I couldn't really tell. She was too scrunched up, too hidden. All hair and elbows. All hoodie.

Garth was also a little thrown by this talk. Maybe Keri had a point. Garth had never seen me play basketball and now he seemed to be considering the likelihood that I wasn't that good. Certainly I'd never gone around talking it up or anything. There was no buzz of scouts around me either, no talk of future prospects. He was also remembering that he was the father of a daughter with qualities. How many times had he sung the praises of his girl? He often used Keri to gauge our shortcomings—if my kid had been here, she would have seen this before it happened. I've got a sixteen-year-old daughter who could do that with her eyes closed.

'You just visiting?' I asked.

Keri didn't look up.

Right then there was a knock on the door and Rachel came in with a plate. 'Pancakes!' she sang out. 'Pancakes! Get 'em while they're hot!' At more or less the same time, the door at the rear of the office opened—it led to a set of stairs that went down to the service entrance and the wheelie bin and the space where Garth parked his car and where there was room for one other vehicle, if it were small enough—and in walked Mr Le Clair.

'Now that's what I call timing,' he said, relieving Rachel of the plate of pancakes and passing his cane to Garth, who stood immediately to receive it with hands that shook slightly; he used the cane to steady himself. He'd been waiting for Mr Le Clair all day probably, but then with the arrival of his daughter, he'd forgotten him. It seemed to have thrown him. 'Have one,' said Mr Le Clair, holding the plate up to me. 'Fuel for the engine.' Immediately he swivelled on his boot heel to face the desk, where Keri was sitting. 'And you,' he said, 'I've heard so much about you. You've come to help out the old man?' Garth went to speak but Mr Le Clair held up his hand. 'What I'm dying for first is coffee.' Garth nodded at Rachel. 'Flat white and four sugars—please don't judge me,' said Mr Le Clair. 'Oh, and bring me one of those heart-disease donuts if Garth hasn't eaten the whole lot. You're so sweet. Isn't she a sweet kid? Anyone else want something? And, honey, take something out, if you would, to my driver. He won't bite. Second thoughts, tell Dave to take it out. He won't bite Dave but with you he could easily get the idea.'

Mr Le Clair drank his coffee and listened to Garth make the explanations. Keri had been shipped here by her mother to achieve a clean break from what Garth called 'stuff'. Aspiring was a great place for a fresh start, he said. New friends, the mountain air, the great outdoors. It occurred to me that none of these items seemed to play any part in Garth's own life. He was old Aspiring, like my old man. Through all this, Keri worked a fingernail into the wood of her father's desk, occasionally looking at her phone.

Mr Le Clair was finishing his donut and wiping the sugar from his waistcoat. 'Welcome, Keri,' he said. 'Your father's completely right. This is a place of great opportunity. Whenever I come, I get a lift from the sound of electric saws and hammers, the snap of architectural drawings in the breeze, the grind of cement mixers. Won't mean much to someone of your age but what this all means is growth. And you're part of that growth.

You know there's a new pool going in, a new school. Forget Auckland, they're building new streets in Aspiring by the month. Doesn't matter what's brought you here. You're here now! You've made a great choice. Even if it wasn't yours. You're ahead of the game, I'd say. The world awaits you. As it does this young man.' He glanced at me. 'How wonderful to be on the edge of all that. Eh, Garth?'

'Oh, yeah, the edge,' said Garth, gloomy. 'Love the edge.'

Mr Le Clair walked over to where I was standing and looked me up and down. Was he calculating whether to measure me again? What was his next prophecy concerning my life? But I had something to ask him. Was this the time? How could I bring up the shoe-store thugs in front of Garth and his daughter? Whisper it?

He was close enough now for me to see the tiny arrow-shaped pin stuck in his lapel. My mouth went suddenly dry. I bent closer. He noticed and moved the lapel so the pin caught the light. 'Like it?' he said.

It was the St Louis arch.

10.

'Do you want to know dates?' said Miss Milton. 'Dates are very boring probably. What sort of thing do you want to know? I've lived a very dull life, I'm warning you. I was twenty-two before I went on a plane. Never had children, which makes it hard to have conversations around here. "The interesting things my children are doing", which often I do find interesting. I can only think of my own childhood, also very boring. I was a happy child. Or not unhappy. My father had a repair business in our converted garage. Heaters, radios, clocks—he could fix anything. My mother worked as a legal typist. It was nothing special. They worked hard and it was just me. Is this the sort of thing you need?'

I nodded and told Miss Milton that hobbies were sometimes a good way to start storifying. It was our teacher's word, I said. What did you like doing when you were young, stuff like that. It was Thursday afternoon and my brain was still stuck somewhere on Wednesday at Pete's.

'Hmm. I liked tennis. Saturday mornings. What else? I remember I got very keen on upholstery at one point. Was I twelve or thirteen? People would drop off their chairs, Dad set me up in one corner of the garage. Was that unusual for a child, more or less, to be an upholsterer? I suppose it was. But still, boring! I wonder if you have the wrong gal, Ricky. There are plenty of fascinating people a few doors down, across the road. I can take you to them. Quite fascinating. A woman who worked for years at Buckingham Palace. Do you know they stack mistresses for the royals in all the big castles? They just live there for years, like staff.'

We were sitting in her little living room, which connected to her little kitchen. A person of average height would have used that adjective. She'd poured me a glass of juice and put out a plate of biscuits. Her teacup was floral, delicate—nothing like the heavy missiles at Pete's. Those cups could bounce off floors unharmed. I didn't really know what upholstery was but it sounded dull and difficult. Miss Clarke had told us that when we interviewed our 'books', we needed to be led by the person and not by our own interests, though—she added—we could certainly keep an ear out for things that would entertain and inform and the book might pass over too quickly. We were editors as well as listeners, she said, but ultimately the human library was about self-description, the books owning their own stories and sharing what was important to them. In truth, when I looked at Miss Milton, all I thought about was the fire that Dad had pulled her and her mother from. But it would have been rude to hurry her along, and anyway, maybe that event wasn't any sort of highlight.

I checked again that my phone was recording and then looked down at my notepad, pretending to write something and making it unreadable so that Miss Milton wouldn't be able to look over and see that I was struggling. After this I was meeting Keri at Clip-and-Climb—her idea. The boss's daughter! That was also where my mind went.

And: *He had a pin of the St Louis arch on his lapel.* How? Why?

The old woman sipped her tea and I drank my juice and reached for another biscuit.

'You'd be hungry all the time, I imagine,' she said.

'Sorry,' I said. My hand was already on the biscuit.

'No, no, I'm being silly, have as many as you like. I don't eat them.'

My munching seemed over-loud in the quiet of Miss Milton's little unit. We both stared out the window, where a neat garden glistened and two birds hopped on the patch of lawn beside a single wooden seat. A mottled stone cat kept guard by the chair but the birds played carelessly around its unmoving shape. Beyond the garden was the golf course. In the distance a group was trundling up a fairway, stopping, hitting, then moving on.

She smiled at me. 'You're thinking about the fire, aren't you, Ricky?'

'No, I was thinking about the upholstery.'

She laughed. 'Of course you were!'

'People bringing their chairs to you.' I leaned forward earnestly, just as I'd seen TV reporters do.

'What a sweet boy you are. Watch out or I'll tell you about the time I re-covered a sofa in velvet.' Miss Milton laughed again. 'I can tell you about the fire.'

'Only if you want to. Maybe you don't want to and that's fine.'

'I don't mind. Your father was absolutely heroic. He saved our lives. That should be *storified*, yes?' Miss Milton had a habit—I saw this now—of lifting her eyes upwards when trying to remember something, as if the thing hovered a few inches above her and could be coaxed down, as if memories were like planes circling, waiting for clearance from the tower. 'Actually, I don't remember much. The mind shuts down, I suppose, in times of stress.'

I nodded again. How hard could it be to recall a few details? I tapped my pen on my notepad.

'Maybe if you asked me questions,' she said.

'Okay. How did the fire start?'

'They think it was the old wiring.'

'It was late at night, wasn't it?'

She paused, placing her cup on its fine saucer. 'Two or three in the morning. I woke up to smoke. Everywhere smoke. You couldn't see a thing. Which way was the bedroom door? My window suddenly shattered, which gave the fire more oxygen. There was a whoosh and my bedroom was lit up. I saw the door finally. But which way to go? Through the window probably. But Mother. I shouted, I think. Yes, I was shouting for her. But the smoke got in my lungs and I was coughing. Stupid to have opened my mouth and called out. Then, amazingly, courageously, your father was there. I have no idea about time. It might have been a few minutes or less. They put me down on the lawn and one thing I remember very clearly—how cool the grass was! How wet!'

Dewy! I thought. The Dewy decimal system.

'I felt it connect with my skin. Also the tremendous noise of the flames. The feeling too that we'd been ... attacked.'

'Attacked by someone? Arson or ...?'

'Just singled out. At that point I thought I was on my own. I mean that my mother wouldn't have survived. She was very old. I wasn't young myself. Her bedroom was near the kitchen and I just thought that was where the fire had probably come from. I had no reason for thinking that. My father had died many years before, and I thought now you are on your own, girl. Now you better shape up. How strange. I thought of the future. Already I had put the house, all our possessions, and my own mother into the past. A new beginning! I'm not proud of those feelings.'

The two birds were at the French doors, flitting about the step, twisting their heads to take us in. I thought of the bird who'd come to the shoe store when I was lying on the floor after being decked by the hoods who were heavying Sim. Why were these birds always around? What did they know? The golfers were close now: two women and two men.

Miss Milton brought her hands down sharply on her knees and stood up. It startled me. 'No, no, this is all wrong for your school project, Ricky. Completely inappropriate. Your father should be the book. He's the real hero. He could tell it with all the details, the excitement and so on.'

'We're not allowed to get our parents. Besides, he wouldn't ever agree.'

She went to the French doors and the birds took off, landing nearby in a little tree—not much more than a collection of twigs—whose trunk was protected by a staked circle of wire mesh. The streets of the retirement village were dotted with these tiny trees. In a few years, everyone said, the plantings would take and the place would be lush and leafy. For now it had a slight after-the-bombing feel, with bare humps of earth signalling buried ordinances. The dips and rises, sprinkled with grass seed, had in fact been patterned by terrifying raids from which there were few survivors. The new inhabitants had no idea and preferred not to dig. *As the plane banked to enter the cloud cover, he caught sight of something out of the corner of his eye. No! How was that even possible? Then he saw the flash of its wings. The enemy was right on his tail!*

'You know there are people in the village who flew fighter planes in the war. I could give you their addresses.'

I stared at Miss Milton. Had she heard me thinking? I hadn't said anything.

She moved to the kitchen sink to rinse her cup and I joined her. We both looked out across the little pretend road at the Aspiring Lifestyle retirement village's croquet lawn, its white

90

hoops looking more like an obstacle course for possums. At night did animals come and jump? This was Bridle Path Lane. I'd come down Rodeo Drive. There was a chipping and putting area around the corner. I realised I had a biscuit in my hand and I slipped it into my pocket. I turned off the recording on my phone and put my notebook and pen into my backpack. I picked up my bike helmet. I wasn't sure where we stood now. Was she out of the human library completely? 'Thank you, Miss Milton.'

She turned back to me. 'Oh, you're going?'

'I thought ...'

'You need to get away.'

'I could ...'

'Only I do have another story.' She sat down in her chair. Through the window she watched one of the men flash at the ball with his club. The jerky motion had clearly not produced the right result. The man stomped his foot in anger and hammered the club into the ground. His companions had already turned and walked on. 'I like to watch them play,' she said. 'I enjoy the drama. Except when the ball lands in my garden or on the roof. Your mother plays, doesn't she?'

'Yes,' I said.

'Dear Michelle, poor Michelle.'

Poor because—? I counted two beats, knowing it was coming.

'Your poor little brother,' she said.

'Big brother,' I said.

Miss Milton smiled and gestured towards the sofa, inviting me to take my seat again. 'Maybe this story is as hopeless as everything else I've told you. You can decide. It's something I've never told anyone. Call me Margaret. Have another biscuit.'

11.

I hadn't done Clip-and-Climb since I was ten or something. We used to go there for birthdays, followed by a meal at the restaurant that was part of the same complex. Paintball was now the go-to. We wanted to shoot each other, then eat pizza. For my sixteenth birthday coming up, I was thinking about just ordering pizza and then having everyone throw the food at each other. Much cheaper.

Keri was waiting by the entrance. I'd texted to say I was running late. Miss Milton's story was still buzzing in my buzzed head. I started apologising and pulling out my wallet but Keri waved a piece of paper unenthusiastically. 'I have a voucher. From Dad. Some deal he has, I don't know. He has all these deals with people in this town. Anyway, we get in for free.'

'Fantastic,' I said.

It had been Garth's idea that we come here. He'd announced it as a thing that was simply going to happen. Was it a date? Keri had been silent, which he took for assent. I'd never much liked climbing and was average at it. Johnny was speedy and sure with his holds. He'd be up and down before I was halfway. I didn't quite see the point of a climbing wall. Up and down, up and down.

The guy handing out the harnesses checked that we'd done it before and then left us to it. We were the only ones there.

It was closing in half an hour. If we'd wanted to, we could have broken all the rules, ditched the safety ropes and climbed like monkeys, fallen like coconuts. From somewhere else in the building, a thumpy bass music sounded as if someone had miked up a person being punched in the stomach. It was an experience still fresh in my body.

'Race?' said Keri. She was already at the wall.

I was still checking all the carabiners. When I looked again, Keri was at the top. 'How'd you do that?' I called up.

She let herself down again, bouncing expertly and lightly with her toes against the wall. 'What kept you?' she said. She took a hair tie from her pocket and swept her hair into a neat ponytail. It was the first proper look I'd had of her face. I can't do faces, where the bits go and what the overall effect is. Garth's daughter, I saw now very clearly, was not a female Garth. She had her mother's influence presumably. What did I look at and like? I looked at the line of her jaw and then her ear. The curve of everything. What else? In this moment she seemed to be allowing me to study her, or at least she didn't care that I looked. Who was I to her? A sort of guard? A tall person to watch over her while her father worked? That might have been what I was to Garth—this was simply an extension of my employment terms at Pete's. Her arms lifted, her chin was thrown back. Make-up covered some bumps at the corner of her mouth. Pimples in exactly the place I got them. Her body looked strong. The lumpy hoodie had been a disguise. She was wearing jeans and a tight Icebreaker top. Her fingers were long and she was flexing them, ready for another climb. At Pete's she'd been hunched. Now she had her shoulders back and her breasts were outlined. She moved along the wall, looking for a different route up.

Being so much taller than everyone, of course it was easier to observe. Not a bird's-eye view exactly, but people seldom felt like checking what I was looking at—they didn't want to crane their necks only to discover I was staring right back.

'You've done this before,' I said.

This time when she launched herself at the wall, I was ready. We reached the top at the same time. Perhaps I was slightly ahead.

'Unfair,' she told me. She looked just a little surprised and admiring.

'What?' I said.

'Daddy long legs!' She laughed.

I reached up and touched the roof. She lifted her own arm but it fell way short.

'How many holds did you need?' she said.

'Don't know.' It was the truth. I'd simply put a hand up and everywhere was a hold. My legs followed and hey presto. It felt like cheating. Another new use of this new body. A good feeling actually.

We hung at the top for a few moments, not talking. Keri pushed herself away from the wall and let the rope slowly turn. Gently revolving, she put her head back, her ponytail dropping behind her, back arching. She'd closed her eyes.

'Can't believe I'm in this shitty place,' she said.

'When it first opened, it was pretty cool. But yeah, it's a bit sad now.'

'Not in here,' she said. 'I meant Aspiring.'

'Oh,' I said.

She continued to turn. 'I mean the blossoms blah blah, the scenery yeah yeah. But. Really? Is that it?'

I didn't know what to say. Aspiring? How could you say that about Aspiring? I felt a prick of loyalty and irritation. 'Yeah,' I said.

She stopped herself spinning and opened her eyes. 'Aren't you supposed to tell me how great it is?'

'Am I? Like, what? Tourism Southern Lakes? Top ten things to do that don't include sitting quietly in a corner, considering the pointlessness of existence in the light of a natural feature as staggering and mysterious as a lake formed millions of years ago?'

She gave me a puzzled look. 'I don't know. Dad thinks you'll be a good influence or something.'

'Oh. Right. Well. Um. Sure.'

She looked at me, smiling. 'Stop with the sales pitch already! I can't bear it! Actually, one thing I've noticed.'

'What's that?'

'There are no fat kids in Aspiring.' She sent herself down to the floor at top speed.

Outside, when I was putting on my bike helmet, Keri said, 'So is that what you think? That existence is pointless?'

'I don't know. I do think we have a "good" lake.'

'Why are you putting quote marks around it?'

I shrugged.

'The lake is fine,' she said. 'Jesus, let's not criticise a lake. If anything, the lake should be criticising us.'

'Yep,' I said. 'And the mountains are pretty cool, too. Not that I have any interest in, you know, going up them. Or down them. Hey, where's your bike?'

'You think I brought a bike down from Auckland?'

'How'd you get here?'

'Dad dropped me off.'

'Oh.'

'Because you guys don't have Uber.' Her phone pinged and she checked it. 'He'll be here in ten minutes. Ten minutes!'

'Wow, you have him wrapped around your finger, eh.'

'No one my age has a bicycle in Auckland. Dads have bikes.'

'Not your dad.'

She gave a short snorty laugh. 'Imagine that!'

'Would you like me to wait until your Uber Daddy comes?'

She shrugged and went to sit on a bench by the entrance. It was dusk and the temperature had dropped suddenly. She hugged herself, rubbing her arms. I wheeled my bike over. She was sitting near the middle of the seat. If I sat down, our legs would almost be touching. Was this what she wanted? For the warmth alone. But I stayed standing, holding my bike. Not many days ago I'd thought holding my bike, wheeling it along with my mates, was one of the great feelings. Now it felt ridiculous, like holding an octopus.

I asked her if she'd heard of the human library idea. She hadn't. Briefly I explained the project. Then I told her about Miss Milton and the fire. Keri seemed only vaguely interested. Even the role of my dad didn't cause her to make more than a grunt. I couldn't help myself—when she made that noise, I laughed.

'What?' she asked.

'You remind me of him.'

'Who?'

'My dad. Like, nothing impresses him.'

'Things impress me,' she said, interested finally in this idea.

'Like what?'

'I don't know.'

'What impresses you?'

'Put me on the spot why don't you. Okay. Beyoncé's stagecraft.'

'Ha!'

'The mind of a cat.'

'The mind of a cat,' I said.

'We can't get inside it. But there are openings from time to time, as if they want us to see something before they close off again. That's insane what they're doing to us.'

'Do you have a cat?'

'He died.' She turned away from me.

It took me a few moments to work out that she was upset. Tough Keri, sniffling about her moggie. I was inches away from telling her about Mikey. Inches. But dead brothers trump dead cats any day and it would have been unfair. 'I'm sorry.'

I heard a car on the main road and thought it might be Garth. It would have been good for him to arrive then and take his daughter away but the car carried on past.

Keri rubbed her eyes and turned back to me. 'I'd be more interested in an animal library than a human library. Humans get way too much attention. Look what they've done to the planet. Whereas animals ...'

'Right,' I said. 'Except, you know, no language.'

'You think?' Her glance was knowing, proud, secretive.

I really didn't want to talk about her dead cat's special mind powers. We fell into a silence. I thought of saying I had to go home now. But I couldn't leave her. Here's the thing: ever since I'd become tall, I felt more gallant. Is that the word? But I also felt other things. Biking along Rodeo Drive in the retirement village, I saw that all the letterboxes were on metal poles at the kerbside of the dinky pretend streets. I had the sudden urge to take a huge sword and strike all the letterboxes down. Off with their stupid heads! Had that thought started with some sentence—*He brandished his sword like the postman of the apocalypse*—then morphed into a real desire? I was a little scared this could be a pattern.

'Miss Milton did tell me something pretty amazing today.'

'Who did?' said Keri.

Oh, come on. 'The old lady I was telling you about, from the fire. She had another story.'

Keri was scrolling through her phone. In the gloom its light picked out her face, the line of her beautifully straight nose. She grinned at something. Maybe she wasn't worth telling the story to. 'Go on,' she said, still thumbing her screen. 'Don't know where Dad is.'

Here's what I told Garth's daughter.

Miss Milton had worked at Greenlane Hospital. At the mention of the hospital, Keri looked up and said, Auckland. Keri was still tuned utterly to her hometown. Yep, I said, Miss Milton, whose name was Margaret, had left Christchurch, where she grew up and trained, and she became a nurse on the surgical ward at Greenlane. She dealt with all kinds of operations.

'Ugh', said Keri.

One day Margaret was assisting in a brain operation.

'Don't,' said Keri. 'Brains! Wait, who's Margaret?'

I asked if Keri was listening and she said she was but I was throwing out these gross terms. Maybe, I said, Keri wasn't ready for this story. But Keri said she was, she was. She just reserved the right to find it all a bit gross, looking inside bodies.

'Anyway,' I started again, 'Margaret was in the surgical theatre.'

'Wearing a mask no doubt,' said Keri with distaste.

'Sure. Mask, gloves, paper hat probably.'

'Ugh,' said Keri.

'And the patient is awake and completely conscious while the operation is taking place. That's normal, Margaret told me, for certain brain operations. It's helpful to have the patient alert.'

'Are you bullshitting me?' said Keri.

'Any time you can avoid a general anaesthetic, go for it,

Margaret said. So, she's talking to the patient while his scalp is open and the surgeons are doing their work.'

'Go away.'

'They crack you open like an egg. Lift the lid. A talking egg.'

'Egghead. Please don't.'

'The patient is given pethidine, which is a sedative. But they're able to talk while their head is flipped open like a—'

'Yeah, yeah,' said Keri, 'we got it now.'

'And this one patient, a man in his sixties according to Margaret, begins to speak softly, drawing her in. Pethidine is known as the truth drug. "I have something important to confess," he tells his nurse. "I have something on my conscience I wish to get rid of."'

Keri had put her phone away now. 'Hey, bend down, will ya,' she told me. 'Your voice is sort of drifting off.'

I squatted down.

'Sit here, dick,' said Keri. 'I mean Rick. Ricky. Are you Richard?'

I moved onto the seat. Our bodies were touching at the hips, along the thighs. 'I have never been a Richard,' I said. 'My dad used to call me Snicko.'

'Before you grew so tall,' she said.

'How'd you know?'

She shrugged. 'Anyway,' said Keri. 'Get on with it.'

'Margaret leans in close to the patient. The doctors are working away up top. Sets of eyes and busy fingers. There's another nurse handing them the tools. Margaret's job is to be with the patient and to monitor vital signs and keep him busy.'

'Keep him busy?' said Keri. 'Like he's going to get bored and wander off.'

'"I haven't told a soul," says the man, the patient.

'"All right, dear," says Margaret. She's used to patients saying odd things or mistaking her for someone else. Pethidine can be a great talker.

'The man takes her hand firmly, drawing her even closer. "Will you listen to this? Something I can't bear any more."

'"Yes, yes, dear," says the nurse. "You're doing great."

'"Something to be rid of, though I never will be rid of it and I don't deserve to be rid of it."

'The nurse pats his hand, "It'll all be over soon. Look how well you're doing."

'The man's head is in a kind of vice to prevent movement. It's delicate up top.'

Keri said, 'They're tweaking his bloody brain! Jesus.'

'The man's eyes drill into Margaret. She's never felt so … *invaded* is the word Margaret Milton used when telling me this story for the human library.'

'She's telling this for the human library?' said Keri. 'This horror story.'

'He grips her hand. "I killed a man," he says. "I murdered a man."

'"What did you do?" asks the nurse, a little frightened now.

'"Did you hear me? I killed someone. And this is my confession. If I don't make it, you'll know everything. If I make it, will you take me to the police? I'm ready to tell them everything, how I did it and why."'

'Holy shit,' said Keri. 'And did she?'

'"I have all the details," the man said. Then he told the nurse everything: names, dates, motive.'

'What had he done?' asked Keri. 'Who'd he kill?'

'Margaret didn't say,' I said.

'Oh, what!' Keri reared away from me, the spell broken.

'Pethidine,' Margaret said. 'You can't trust anything anyone says under the influence.'

'But she believed him?' said Keri. 'She knew, right? He was telling the truth. He was a murderer.'

We both heard Garth's car turning in.

'She told me it's always haunted her,' I said. 'And she's just this little old lady living in a retirement village.'

Keri stood up. 'You have officially freaked me out. I'm not going to be able to sleep. What are you doing tomorrow?'

'I have school. Don't you have school?'

'They chucked me out. That's why I'm down here, while they work out who wants me the most, or dislikes me the least. You know. Ping and pong. Do you have brothers and sisters?'

I shook my head.

'Right,' she said. 'So you know how it can go. They're on opposite sides of the net and you're the ball, yeah.'

'Right,' I said. 'My folks are still together. Just.'

'Lucky you,' said Keri. She turned her head away from me. 'Where's Sticky Forest?'

'What?' I said.

'Sticky Forest.'

'It's round the other side of the lake. Up past school.'

'What happens there?'

'What happens there?'

'Yeah,' she said. She was looking at the ground.

'I don't know. Heaps of mountain biking and stuff. Trails.'

'Trails.'

'Right.'

'Okay,' she said.

I stood up. My shoulders were sore. I'd done something to them climbing. Stretched ligaments that hadn't been stretched, even in basketball.

Keri picked up my bike helmet from the ground and passed it to me. 'Save you making the long trip down, eh.'

'Thanks,' I said.

She looked up at me. 'Who's the current king and queen of Sticky Forest?'

'I don't know,' I said.

'Don't know or not telling?'

Her dad's car was alongside us. Garth's car window opened. 'I hope you young people got some good exercise in there.'

12.

When I got home Mum was cooking dinner and Dad was in the garage with the Camaro. Mum wore an even deeper tan. Her bare arms glowed. I mentioned it and she cut me off. 'Not now, Ricky,' she said. 'All I want to do is come home and be free of criticism. It would be so nice if I could look forward to my family supporting me for a change.'

'Whoa, all right, all right,' I said.

'Wouldn't that be something.'

Perhaps they'd had an argument. It was the cycle, easy to recognise, impossible to stop. The October engine starting up. Every year was the same as my brother's anniversary drew nearer. Now, when Dad fiddled with his prize car, tuning it and tuning it, I thought he was tuning his bad mood, matching it to Mum's deepening darkness, of which the tan was the outward sign.

I went to my bedroom and lay across the floor with my headphones on. Kendrick. I thought of all the things I hadn't told them about: the fifty bucks, Le Clair with his St Louis pin, getting punched in the shoe store, Miss Milton's nursing story, and now Keri. It was suddenly boring that my parents had their own squabbles, their private fights. It was boring that they had a son called Mike who'd been killed in a car accident.

Another thing they didn't know: I smuggled Mum's iPad into the upstairs bathroom where, as Sim liked to say, I liked to *take my relief.* I think he got the saying from a book. Why did I need to do it like this? Why couldn't I think of my leg touching Keri's? Or her fingers when they brushed mine as she handed me my bike helmet? Real girls. Real life. But today, anyway, was different. I found myself on another kind of search: the world's deadliest construction projects. What the hell? It was true. I thought of the man explaining things to us up in the arch a few years before. Let's see then. No one died when the Chrysler Building went up—but how many were supposed to? How many were in the Halfway to Hell club? The Eiffel Tower: one death. Empire State Building: five. World Trade Center: sixty. Two carpenters and a steel erector were killed while building the Auckland Harbour Bridge, which was opened in 1959. Oh, and in Qatar, ahead of the 2022 World Cup, more than nine hundred construction workers had already lost their lives. What the hell! I skimmed the story. At that rate, by the time of kick-off, four thousand will have died. Most of them migrant workers from Nepal and India.

Suddenly I didn't much feel like my usual.

This was the only room from which you could see a tiny piece of the lake. Not long ago I had to go up on my toes to see it. Now I had to bend down to the window. Every day, for some reason, I felt this need to look at the lake, even if it was only for a moment. I was required to check in on the lake. While everything else moved, the lake remained. Was that it? But the lake moved, too. It got warmer. It receded. Now even the lake failed to reassure me. Last summer old people had stood up to their waists in the water, declaring it very pleasant. It had been like a bath and only waist-deep for a hundred metres or more. Meanwhile, not too far away, toxic algal bloom had closed rivers.

At dinner Dad asked me about the Caddy. This was unusual. I was surprised he'd even remembered what I'd told him. It was days ago. Maybe because it was to do with cars. Maybe he knew it would annoy Mum to mention this at the dinner table.

'I haven't seen it recently,' I said. Which was true if recently meant in the past twenty-four hours.

Mum, who'd been quiet, asked how it had gone with Miss Milton and I told her there was plenty of material but organising it could be tricky. The next stage was I would present the 'books' with edited transcripts of what they'd said about their lives and suggest ways of shaping them into brief coherent stories.

'Beginning, middle, and end,' said Dad.

'But,' I said, 'where's the beginning? Birth? First day at school? First job? Marriage? And the end hasn't happened yet, has it? Mostly it all feels like middle to me.'

Mum looked at me. 'Probably, hon, you're making this too complicated.'

Dad was stabbing penne with his fork as if the pasta was alive, then not alive. He'd killed it. Next he was chasing the tomato sauce around his plate. The sauce was blood from the stabbing. 'Yep, too complicated again. Don't overthink it. People overthink things around here.'

Again, this didn't seem to have much to do with me or the subject we were discussing. Mum sighed loudly.

'But what would *your* story be like?' I said. 'Imagine you're a book. Tell me the first sentence. Mum?'

'Oh, I'm not a writer.'

'Neither is Miss Milton. No one's a writer, that's the point. But everyone's life is, you know, a book.'

Dad made a noise. 'Some people you can read like a book.'

'Well,' said Mum, 'I could tell you your father's first line.'

'Really?' said Dad. 'I want to hear this.' He put his loaded fork in his mouth.

'No,' I said, 'you can't tell other people's stories. That's the whole point.'

Mum ignored me. She spoke into the ceiling in a pretend male voice—a monotone. 'My life really began when I set sail from New Zealand for the first time in the engine room of the HMNZS *Waikato* in 1985 and it ended when that frigate was sunk on the twelfth of November—'

'Eleventh,' said Dad through his food.

'—was sunk on the eleventh of November 2000 to become an artificial reef for recreational divers. The end.'

'It's as good a story as any,' said Dad. 'She was a good boat, *Waikato*.'

'See,' said Mum.

We ate in silence.

'What's the middle then?' I said.

'The middle,' said Dad, 'is *this*, I suppose. It's you.' He waved his fork in the air as if he was about to say more but then his head dropped to his plate again.

Mikey, I thought. He was thinking about my brother. That's why he couldn't speak. The middle was also Mikey. This was our Oktoberfest. Here it came, with all its scripted parts.

Mum, not catching this switch or not caring about it, said, 'And we're honoured to play a small role in this great maritime adventure.'

Dad's head shot up again. 'Whereas your mother's story—'

'Here we go, yes,' said Mum.

'It would be about—'

'Listen to this, everyone,' Mum said. 'This'll be good.'

'Well, fair's fair,' said Dad, 'you had your turn. You had your go at me.'

'Oh, right, fair's fair, is it? Right.'

I stood up from the table. 'Can you please stop this now!' I said. 'I can't bear it. I just can't!'

My parents stared at me in silence. I'd never spoken like this before. They looked at me as if I were a stranger.

Then we heard a voice calling out and Auntie Rena walked in. 'Oh, family dinner. Lovely. Don't mind me. Finish, finish! Please sit down, Ricky.'

It was a complete shock. Why now? What had drawn her to us right at this moment? She never came to the house. That was the arrangement.

'What am I doing, busting in on you like this?' she said. 'How terrible! Isn't it terrible, Steve?'

My dad looked at her carefully.

'Actually,' said Rena, 'I have some good news. Last week I went for an audition.'

We couldn't quite understand what she was saying since we hadn't yet returned from whatever brink we'd been on. Who was she again?

'Yes,' she went on, 'and I heard today that I have a part.'

'In what?' said Mum, making the effort finally.

'Just a little show. Dunedin rep theatre thing. Musical theatre. It's nothing.'

'Oh,' said Mum, 'congratulations.'

'It's all amateur.'

'Which you said you'd never do,' said Mum.

'Yes, but look at me now,' said Rena. She did a little twirl.

'I'm pleased,' said Mum.

'I just thought what am I doing with my talent?'

'Nothing,' said Dad.

'Nothing!' said Rena. 'Correct, Steve.'

'I didn't know you wanted to do something with your talent, Rena,' said Mum.

'Oh, love,' said Rena. 'Nor did I. But it turns out I do. I do. Isn't that strange? Isn't that strange, Ricky? How we change.'

I shrugged and Rena laughed.

'Would you like to have a cup of tea?' said Mum.

Rena clapped. 'Celebrate in style! A cup of tea!'

'I think she's already had a few cups of tea,' murmured Dad.

'No,' said Rena, 'what I would like to do, *love* to do, is sing you a song.'

'Now?' I said.

'Now,' said Rena.

'Shall we do the dishes first?' said Dad.

'No, we shan't,' said Mum. 'Leave the dishes. We have to listen to Rena sing her song.'

'Oh, I should leave, I suppose,' said Rena. 'Yes I should. Leave and not sing my song. But, you know, too many people … for whatever reason … they don't get to sing their song!'

'Because they can't sing,' murmured my dad.

'Where shall we sit?' I began to ask but Rena had already started.

Beautiful dreamer, wake unto me
Starlight and dewdrops are waiting for thee …

With the first two lines, Mum let out a gasp as if she'd been winded. Without warning Rena went up a notch, putting everything into it, though without effort.

Gone are the cares of life's busy throng
Beautiful dreamer, awake unto me
Beautiful dreamer, awake unto me …

I felt myself gulp. Rena's singing voice had nothing to do with her normal one. I'd heard her humming around her house, singing a few lines here and there, but only casually. This was different. Suddenly she had power from nowhere. The chorus was too loud for our kitchen. The words came at us on a wave. It was glorious. Tears rolled down Mum's cheeks and she let them. It was all about us and for us but at the same time it seemed we didn't matter and that Rena was only singing for herself, from inside her self. It was as if we shouldn't be looking or listening but that looking and listening was the one thing we owed her. I could hardly breathe. I didn't know what was happening.

Beautiful dreamer, out on the sea …

At that point Dad stood up and left the room.

Later that evening I went out to the garage. I felt a sting of disloyalty to Mum. Why talk to the old man?

Because I was stupid. Clearly.

Dad was still working on the electrics of the Camaro. The radio was on. Someone was talking about telescopes. He turned it down. I told him I'd looked up the HMNZS *Waikato*. What Mum had said. Vaguely I knew the story but I'd never bothered to find out more.

I said, 'In 1990 it went to Bougainville.'

'Yep,' said Dad.

'You were on that trip?'

'I was.'

'Operation Big Talk.'

'That's the one.'

'You were the venue and accommodation for everyone involved in some peace talks.'

'Port Kieta.'

'What was that like?'

'Hot.'

'I didn't really know where Bougainville was … is.'

'PNG.'

'Or where that was.'

He continued to fiddle with the pliers. Barely audible, the voice on the radio said, *In fact the night sky is now full of more mysteries. The mysteries don't diminish but multiply in response to the sophistication of our tools.* A few moments went past.

'Operation Big Talk,' I said. 'Lucky someone else had to do the talking.'

He looked at me then. 'I didn't see much of up top, Ricky. Just a lot of important people, you know. The catering went up a notch. Everything went up a notch. Linen, alcohol, whatever. We were more or less floating hotels. They had their job in the meeting rooms and I had mine down below. We were there with the *Endeavour* and the *Wellington*. A week or something.'

'Nine days.'

'There you go.'

'You know you can apply for a medal.' According to the website, the announcement had been made the previous year.

'Yep.'

'Are you going to?'

'Nope.'

'Why not?'

'I was just doing my job.'

'An important job.'

'There were lots of us. I wasn't special.'

'But it's an achievement. It's recognition. It's part of history.'

'Oh, well, we're all part of history. And what would I do with this medal? I'm not going to hang it on the wall.'

'Why not?'

'For people to look at?'

I laughed. 'Why not, Dad?'

He put his head down again to twist at something under the dash. 'At the barber's, when he cuts my hair, I look down and see all this grey stuff. It's always a big surprise. Who the hell does that belong to! Turns out that's my hair. That's me on the floor. Sure, I'm part of history.' He began working the wires again. I started walking to the door. 'She's gone is she, your aunt?'

'Ages ago.'

'Good singer.'

'Amazing.'

'Really good. I'd kind of forgotten.'

'Why'd you leave, Dad? You walked out.'

'Ha, things to do, you know.' He looked down at his pliers. 'Listen, no one wants to see a grown man reduced to a blubbering wreck.'

I nodded. I wouldn't have minded seeing that.

He looked at me. 'You're ...' He couldn't finish whatever he wanted to say.

'What's that?'

'You're different, Ricky.'

'From?'

'From before. You're changing.'

'Growing.'

'No, not just that ... It's something to see. Everything okay?'

I almost burst out laughing. Or crying. But no one wants to see a blubbering wreck. 'Yeah.'

'Good. Okay. Thinking about the big game, I suppose.'

'Yeah.'

'You'll do well, I'm sure. You're a well-prepared outfit.'

'Yep.'

'Okay, Snicko. That is all.' He grinned at me, waving his pliers in farewell.

'Want me to hold some wires?'

'Nope.'

'Dismissed?' I asked.

'Dismissed,' said my dad.

13.

Ahead of the play-off, Coach Dennett had arranged a closed-session Friday night practice game against a senior men's team from Dunedin. They were coming up in a minivan and word was they were going to destroy us and then destroy the town and finally destroy the minivan.

I had to ask Garth if I could leave work early that evening. He told me I shouldn't have come in at all. I should be preparing. 'The regionals!' he said.

'But Friday's a busy night,' I said.

'And you're so essential to the successful management of that increased customer flow?' He slapped me on the back. 'Get outta here! You're a vital cog on that team, buddy. Go inflict some damage on those simpletons from the south.'

Keri was waitressing alongside Rachel. When I was packing up my stuff, she came through into the kitchen. She had her hair tied back and looked much older. Make-up. Girls were lucky like this. They could become someone else in the blink of an eye or however long it took to apply the make-up. A boy was made of the same putty all the time. Our faces were bland, dull as pieces of dough. No wonder we wanted to punch each other, rearrange our noses and make our eyes balloon and rainbow. No wonder we ground each other's faces into the mud. We hoped to see something different, something changed. We wanted to be girls or for girls to stare at us and say, I didn't see that coming.

Of course we grew up and out. Hairs. Muscle. Bulge. And now voices—suddenly as if we'd swallowed rats.

'Look at you,' said Keri.

'What?' I said.

'So serious.'

'No,' I said.

She laughed. 'He's thinking about the game. Game face.'

'Hardly,' I said. 'It's just a friendly. A practice game.'

'No such thing,' she said. She landed the tray of glasses she was carrying on the stainless-steel bench in front of me with a great clatter. I'd noticed there was nothing careful in her waitressing moves. She blundered about, knocking things over, getting orders wrong, careless and unapologetic, making a point of the servitude she was suffering in her father's restaurant. Keri wasn't at all the model worker Garth was always describing to make us feel bad. She was sort of an oaf. More or less the bench had intervened before the tray of glasses hit the ground. Maybe he'd lied. But then it occurred to me that maybe she'd changed—changed from when she was his star. She was a different thing now. Like me.

'Leaving me with all the work, eh,' she said.

'I have permission,' I said.

'From his majesty.'

'From Garth the magnificent,' I said.

Keri laughed at this. She flicked at a small food mark on the breast pocket of her white blouse. But it didn't come off.

'You're letting this establishment down,' I said. 'The state of that shirt.'

'Why are you looking at my shirt?'

Because I want to take it off. 'I wasn't.'

'Why are you going red, Ricky?'

'The heat from the kitchen,' I said.

'If you can't stand the heat.'

We looked at each other. Then Logan was calling out a table number. 'Service!' Keri turned away, scooped up two meals, and went through into the restaurant.

The ball game against the older dudes from Dunedin was brutal. We started well and were up by twelve after the first quarter. We were moving it nicely through the court. Johnny, with his dribbling and hard low passing, was particularly good against their bigger players. Angus too was finding plenty of room in the circle. Sim, even with his sore foot, was too quick for most of their players. I'd got some rebounds and two points from the free-throw line. Then they adjusted. Suddenly our offence was slowed. They picked up three-pointers. I couldn't get under the hoop to compete for the loose stuff. There was this crowd, a forest of limbs in my face. I was used to seeing over the top of all that. Our lead vanished. I didn't know what was happening until Coach Dennett drew lines on his mini whiteboard on a timeout. 'They're teaming Johnny!' he said. 'They've compressed their D. We've got to vary our supply.' He pointed the marker pen at me and drew a mad series of criss-crossing lines on the board. 'Clemens, you're not playing statues out there. Movement!' The lines were evidently me, moving.

Our opposition knew all the tricks. Hardly any decision went unquestioned by them. In twos and threes they ran to the ref. But they smiled as they complained, holding their hands behind

115

their backs. *Excuse me.* Reasonable. Somehow they managed it that Sim was fouled off in the third quarter ahead of any number of their own offenders getting terminally pinged. They had two guys who were about an inch shorter than me but this pair was bigger all over. Their shoulders would swivel suddenly and I was on the floor. It happened again and again as the game went on. I laughed the first time. One minute I was defending with my arms up and then I was sliding across the floor on my butt. I stopped laughing after that and tried to remember the whiteboard me, the wonderful guy zipping about, up and down the court, up and down, tireless and inspired. Johnny was yelling at me. 'Available! Be available!' I got an elbow in the face. My feet were stamped on at every opportunity. I was too available. At an early fourth-quarter timeout, down by sixteen points, Coach benched me. 'You're done, Clemens. Sit down.'

We actually came back a little and the loss in the end was by ten. Their captain came over and congratulated us, wishing us luck. He seemed like a good guy. In fact they were all fine. A couple of them were carrying babies after the game, chatting to their partners. Others held the hands of their little kids, who'd sat through the game playing on devices. The player who'd sat me on my arse most often shook my hand and asked if I was going to Otago when I finished school. He knew a team that needed a bit of height. I told him I hadn't thought that far ahead. I asked what they were doing now. It turned out most of them were heading back to the lodge they'd booked to get their kids to bed. Then they had to be back in Dunedin early the next day. Oh, okay. No one was up for destroying Aspiring that night.

Coach Dennett had quickly converted the loss into a learning. 'That, gentlemen,' he told us, 'was very very useful. Why was it useful?' He looked around the changing room. 'Anyone?'

Johnny put up his hand. 'If we have to adjust mid-game, we need a plan B.'

'Correct!' Then there was a lot of talk about what our plan B was and how we might implement it and at what point in a game we should make the switch. Having only a shaky grasp of our plan A, I waited out this conversation, making sure I nodded thoughtfully whenever a statement came my way. To be honest, watching the last bit of the game from the bench had been a highlight for me. Free from the anxiety of actually playing, I'd begun to enjoy the skills on show. More and more, I saw how clearly my own contributions against good opposition would hold our team back. My height had reached its limits if not its height. This was the idea I was formulating as the others agreed on tactics heading into the play-off. I'd go to Coach and tell him not to play me. I'd tell him what I'd seen and what surely he'd seen in that final quarter, without me muddying the waters, stuffing things up. We both knew the deal. Time to cut me loose. Warming the pine, I'd seen my future and it was not in wearing the number five singlet. A nice feeling flowed through me as I thought of us shaking hands. I'd have to look a little regretful and sad but also grateful. I'd come a long way ...

Then I became aware that Coach Dennett was close to me, talking directly into my ear.

'Hello? Hello in there?' he said.

'Coach?' I said.

'Did you hear what I just said, Clemens?'

'Plan B,' I said.

'After that.'

'Plan ... C?' I said. The guys laughed.

'I said some people stood up tonight to some fairly punishing stuff.'

'Oh,' I said. 'Sure. They were amazing.'

'Not they, Ricky,' he said. 'Not just *they*. I mean *you* took a beating. Thrown on your arse. Assaulted. Provoked. Man-handled, I'd say, by those pricks.'

'What? Nah, they were okay.' I rubbed the side of my face and winced—it was swollen from the elbow jab.

'Jesus, see what I mean? You took it and you got back up, Clemens.'

Some of the boys said yeah. Yeah you did.

'Well, you can't just lie around, Coach.'

'If you did nothing else in the entire game—and you came close to that, to be fair—but if you did nothing else, Clemens, you did that. *You got back up.* To progress to the regionals, we're going to need that kind of spirit. Am I right?'

'You're right, Coach,' said Johnny loudly.

'Coach!' said Angus, banging his own thigh in agreement.

'We need more of what Clemens showed!' said Coach Dennett.

'That's a bit much,' I said.

'Yeah!' shouted the boys. 'Clemens!'

Coach took off his cap and slapped it against his knee. 'Some ugly bunch of dipshits try to take over our court, push us around, throw us to the floor—what do we do?'

'Get up like Clemens!' they all yelled. Then they started a chant, clapping out the words. 'Up like Clemens! Up like Clemens! Up like Clemens!'

It was really embarrassing and stupid.

We got a lift home with Johnny's dad, and Johnny and Sim kept up the bullshit, saying how I'd stood strong against the viciousness of the opposition. I kept waiting for them to wink at me, but they never did. Obviously they needed to hang on to something ahead of the play-off game and this was it: my heroism. Finally, I thought oh, well, if this is my only contribution to the team, then I'll have to live with it. Sucks at basketball but not a cry-baby.

14.

Saturday morning Mum knocked on my door. 'Someone to see you, Ricky.'

'Who?' I was in bed. I was sore from last night's game.

'Keri.'

What the hell? 'Okay, out in a minute.' I got dressed as fast as I could, washed my face—ouch—brushed my teeth, ran down the stairs. Mum was at the kitchen bench. We could see Keri waiting out the front of our house, holding a bike. For a moment it was as if we were looking at a complete foreigner. Or at the future. And we both were wondering, oh, dear, what can we do?

'I asked her in,' said Mum, 'but she said she was fine and you had to get going. On your bike ride.'

'Right,' I said.

'Who is she, Ricky?'

'New girl.'

'From school.'

'From Pete's.'

'How old is she?'

I drank a glass of water and put the glass on the bench. 'Gotta go, Mum.'

'What about breakfast?'

'I'm good.'

Outside I told Keri I'd get my bike from the garage. She nodded and put on her helmet.

Soon we were riding off down the street in the direction of the lake. I pulled alongside her. 'Did you text me or something about this?'

'Did you not get it?'

'No.'

'Hmm,' said Keri. 'Maybe I didn't text you.' She pulled away, pushing hard on her pedals.

I caught her up again. It was easy enough. My legs went around. The seat, even at its maximum extension, wasn't high enough but it was okay. I forgot about the basketball knocks and bruises. I called out, asking where we were going, but she didn't turn her head or answer. The wind was blowing my words back into my face. The lake was greenish today, choppy, with pale ridges — the whole thing like a cabbage leaf.

We crossed the road and biked along the lakeside path, past the playground with its elephant slide, where parents sipped their takeaway coffees while their children ran around. The elephant's trunk had once been a fully enclosed tube. Before I was born, my brother had become trapped with four other children inside this trunk. One of the kids had apparently refused to either go down or come back up and Mikey had been one of a group who'd careened into him. There was screaming and panic. A father tried to reach up inside the trunk but he was too big. Wedged in, he had to be rescued by another father. It was a complete circus, Mum said. She loved telling the story. She'd been calling to Mikey to stay calm. Finally an older child had crawled inside the trunk and pulled them all out. But after that ruckus the trunk had been deemed a hazard and, as a safety measure, its sides were cut open. I never went past the playground without thinking of my brother trapped inside the slide. There was no damage done, though from that point on, Mikey refused to read his Babar books.

I thought of telling Keri this story but she was already whizzing past the family groups. She almost took out a toddler. I called out for her to slow down.

By the boat ramp I pulled alongside her again. Her riding wasn't as furious now. 'Where'd you get the bike?'

'This town is made of bikes,' she said. 'But no one coasts along, do they. They go hard. Everyone's training for something, trying to beat something, personal bests. That's how you do it, right? Go hard, Ricky!' And she took off again.

But now we had to slow down, almost coming to a stop, to allow a trailer carrying a boat to reverse towards the ramp. The driver had his head out the window, checking on progress. It was Angus's father. He saw me and waved. I waved back.

'Everyone knows everyone,' said Keri. It was a criticism. Then, while I was still waiting for Angus's dad to pass, she accelerated around the car, heading on to the bush track, disappearing through the trees. For a non-biker she had a lot of confidence.

I almost missed her when the track turned away from the lake. But I caught a flash of something down by the water: her red helmet, which she was taking off. I doubled back and pushed my bike onto the stony beach, leaving it beside hers. 'Almost lost you,' I said.

She lay back and put her arms over her eyes, shading herself from the sun. I saw her chest was rising and falling quickly. She was stuffed.

'Hey, you all right, Keri?'

'Shit I hate biking,' she said, sitting up.

'You were really going for it.'

'I'm sore all over. Why didn't you tell me to slow down?'

'I tried!'

'Now I think I'm dying.'

'Take it easy for a while. You'll be fine.'

She had her phone out and turned her back to the lake for a selfie. Then she said, 'Why are you grinning like that?'

'Sorry.'

'But why?'

'It was just your selfie face.'

'I don't have a selfie face.'

'Exactly. It's the same face. Just your regular face.'

'Pissed off. Glum. Hostile. Yeah, I know.'

'It's cool.'

'It's not cool, Ricky. It's not a thing.'

'Right,' I said. 'But that's what's cool.'

She shook her head. 'Easily impressed.'

'I also like Beyoncé's stagecraft,' I said.

Out on the lake we watched a boat pulling a waterskier. The skier crossed the wake of the boat and performed a jump with a 360-degree rotation, landing it perfectly. 'Yeah, yeah,' said Keri.

'You know,' I said, 'life is possible without light and even oxygen. There are creatures who live without them. But all life needs water.'

'All waterskiers need water,' she said.

'And all jet-skiers need a bullet,' I said.

She laughed. 'How old are you anyway? Hard to tell.'

'Sixteen next month.'

'Next month! Oh, boy.'

'Why?'

She shook her head.

'I know you're sixteen.'

'And a half. I'm the older woman.'

We looked out at the lake again, where the boat with the skier was now far across the other side.

'I thought you were working today,' I said.

'Not on till four.'

'Hey, who is Mr Le Clair? Do you know? How does he fit in with your dad?'

'He's a creep.'

'A creep who does what? They do business or something?'

'No idea.'

'I think …'

She glanced over at me. 'What do you think?'

'Nah,' I said.

'You think something. I want to know.'

I said, 'I think he's from another world.'

It just fell out. Like one of those private sentences I had looping. Except this was what I believed. Take it back, I told myself. Save yourself! *Take it back right now!* But it was too late.

She let out a short laugh. 'They're a good pair then. Because my dad is definitely from another world.' She looked at me again. 'What do you mean? You serious?'

I shrugged. Was I serious? Until I said it, I had no idea I thought it. But once it was out, I had to agree: this is what I think. Not the crime world. Something else.

'What other world?' Keri asked.

'I don't know,' I said. *Take it back, fool!* 'I'm not serious! I'm not being serious.'

'Right,' she said, studying me, beading right into me. 'You just love saying crazy shit. You go around all the time making up stuff to appear more interesting. You want to be more visible, eh. It's how you roll.'

'Maybe.' My heart was beating hard and in an irregular pattern.

'Ricky, you're a hundred feet tall! You don't need visibility enhancement. You stoop to be smaller. You sit down whenever you enter a room to disappear. And you don't say much at all. Because then people would have to find where the noise came from. And you don't want to be found. Now this? Mr Le Clair is from another world? Listen, wanna know something crazy? I believe in God. The minute you say you believe in God, well anything goes, right? I think all of this ...' she gestured towards the lake, the mountains, the sky, 'all of this, I believe, somehow came from the mind of God, though I don't know what that is, strictly. How to comprehend it. But admit to that, and you've got to allow that some creepy dude in a string tie with slicked-back hair might just be from the spirit world.'

'Spirit world! Yes,' I said. 'Is that a thing?'

'It's in the realm of possible things, I'd say. But like I said, I have no real idea. I can't even stay in school. I can't even hold a beaker over a Bunsen burner without wanting to create an explosion.'

'Is that what you did?'

'That was one of the things I did. That was tiny. And learning related. But we're off-topic. What's Le Clair done to signal his other-worldliness?'

I told her then about the silver pin Le Clair wore and our family's connection to the Gateway Arch and the man on the viewing platform who'd told us about the thirteen men who were supposed to lose their lives. I didn't tell her about Mikey. I told her about the short black Caddy driving near our house, the measuring of my height. I told her about how he'd predicted stuff: buying booze for those guys, getting punched in the shoe store. It didn't really add up as I told it. I could see Keri was trying to follow the trail. Was there a trail? It was all random, wasn't it? Coincidence. I was probably going too fast—way ahead of her, disappearing from view just as she'd disappeared from me on the bike.

'Okay. Step by step,' she said. 'Can I walk it through? Let's see. They bet on your height because it's just a stupid game between them.'

'Right,' I said.

'Le Clair has this weird car because, I don't know, it fits his weird personality. Le Cadillac. Vanity. Who knows.'

'He hangs with your father because?'

'He hangs with my father because … let's park that. Garth is not from the spirit world, that's all I know. He's Garth. He's of this world with a vengeance.'

'Okay. And the pin on Le Clair's lapel? The arch pin?'

'He's from there? Coincidence? I don't know.'

'Coincidence. Yes, I thought of that.'

'You're allowed to have coincidence. What else? The predicting thing. I think I could have predicted that stuff. People can be arseholes. They don't like things out of the mean, beyond the average. They want you cut down to size. You're a tall poppy. A tall Ricky.'

'That's true.'

'Is there anything else?'

'What do you mean?'

'Is there something else?'

'Mikey,' I blurted, not meaning to. Not knowing exactly why. Keri looked blank. 'Who?'

'Mikey was my older brother who died. Car accident.'

'Okay,' said Keri. 'Sorry.'

When she said that simple word, a huge crushing feeling washed up through me. I shuddered. When I tried to speak, I couldn't. Keri waited. Why was she waiting? Finally, I managed to say a word. 'Ten.'

Still she waited.

'He was ten,' I said. That was better. 'I was only five. I didn't really know him.'

'That's sad as. Your poor parents.'

I nodded, afraid again I'd lose it if I tried to speak.

She said, 'What's the Le Clair connection?'

'Don't know.' I picked up a stone and chucked it into the lake. 'Thirteen people were supposed to die in the construction of the Gateway Arch. My grandfather didn't die. He came home and had a family and lived a long life. But Mikey didn't live a long life. What if Le Clair is tied up in that?'

'But how?'

'Yeah,' I said. 'How?'

Keri was looking at the ground.

'All of it,' I said, 'sounds like some crazy shit.'

'I think we've established that crazy shit isn't to be ruled out in this universe,' she said. 'Unbelievable things happen all the time. How did the two of us end up here for instance?' She stood up suddenly. 'So, can you give me a ride on your bike?'

'Oh,' I said. 'Sure. I haven't done that for a while. Not since—'

'Not since you were a kid. Don't worry, I can make it, I think.'

I picked up a stone and looked at it. 'Does this ride have a destination?'

Keri looked at me quickly, then turned away. She was rubbing her calves. 'Don't you know?'

In the end she rode her own bike but more sedately, and we made frequent short stops. Neither of us had brought a water bottle or any snacks. The morning was warm and our riding made us warmer as we climbed slowly up the steeper streets above the lake. Her face was flushed. I could feel sweat behind my knees, down my back. It took us another hour to reach the small carpark by the entrance to Sticky Forest.

She looked up at the bare hillside above us, the track snaking into a line of scrubby low trees. 'This?' she said. 'This is it?' We sat down on the grass.

There were several cars parked by here. Three guys in their late twenties were securing their mountain bikes to the back of a Land Cruiser. They had mud spray up their backs. They were laughing, talking about the ride they'd just had. When the bikes were attached, they changed out of their dirty gear, walking around the car in their underpants, wiping themselves with towels. Occasionally they looked up at us. When they were dressed they drove off.

'It's just a place for mountain biking,' I said stupidly. 'There are all these trails with jumps and stuff. It's for trailheads.'

She took out her phone and lay back on the grass.

I wanted to check my phone, too, but something was stopping me. I thought if I take out my phone, this will end now. But what will end now? From somewhere deep inside Sticky Forest, we heard distant shouting, whooping, then it faded out. I said, 'What do you want to do now?'

She sighed. 'Oh, Ricky Ricky Ricky.' She tried to take off her sneakers by using her feet while still looking at her phone.

I moved below her and took one of her feet in my hands. I undid the laces and eased her shoe off. I did the same with her other foot. She let me. I felt her feet moving in my hands.

'I wouldn't get too close down there,' she said. 'I must stink.'

'I stink, too, so what's the difference.'

She lifted her head and smiled at me. Then she put her head back on the grass. But she'd put her phone down and she was staring up at the sky. 'Have you ever played what cloud are you?'

'No,' I said.

'Me neither. Shit I have no idea how to be romantic.' She shouted a laugh at the sky.

'Me neither.' It hit me suddenly: does she think I have a condom? And: why don't I have a condom? I had a condom hidden in my bedroom. They came from an older guy at school. Or rather Sim had stolen them from the guy, then handed them out to me and Johnny. A johnnie for Johnny. Originally I had two but in the interests of testing, I'd used one solo.

Keri said, 'If I'd texted, maybe you would have come up with an excuse.'

'Why would I have come up with an excuse?'

'I don't know. Because … *this*. Shit, I'd make up an excuse to avoid going on a bike ride with me.'

'You aren't the one who thinks his life is being invaded by malevolent beings.'

'No! No, I always think that.' Keri sat up at once. She was very serious. 'I'm just not used to having company. Let's go back now.' She stood up quickly, shoving her feet into the sneakers. 'I can't stop thinking about them. Le Clair. And your brother. Sorry.'

'Nah,' I said, 'forget about that. It was just because I'm a bit dehydrated. And I haven't eaten. I missed breakfast. I just need to drink something and eat something. Then I'll be better.' I was still speaking when she was beginning to ride off.

15.

The world contracted, expanded, started emitting wheezing sounds like a broken piano accordian someone was pressing between their knees. If only he could find the source of this song, the owner of this horrible instrument …

Closer to the play-off, my internal commentary revved up, got weirder.

I was trying to listen to Mr Wilson for the human library project. His voice had become a drone of dates and names and figures and calculations and near things. 'I tell you, it was a near thing.' I was thinking if I had a band, it would be called The Near Things. Sim had had drum lessons. Johnny had an acoustic guitar. I longed to check whether there was already a band with that name. But my phone was on the coffee table between us, recording Mr Wilson. We were sitting in his overheated lounge at the retirement village, the sun striking his ears from behind, making them glow like the elements in a toaster, the radiator sizzling away. I felt my head jerk a few times and I had to sit up to stop nodding off. Mr Wilson didn't seem to notice. He was telling me about a time when some crisis was narrowly averted at the water-treatment plant near Christchurch. It involved testy phone calls, a late-night car ride, a torch that kept cutting out, a faulty gauge, another close call … The Close Calls?

To stay with it, I would pick up my phone from time to time and check that it was recording. But this also had the effect of stopping Mr Wilson mid-speech—'in case you miss anything'—and then he'd start the engine again, tailing back to earlier points in the narrative 'so you're up to speed'.

Finally the story appeared finished. Mr Wilson looked at his watch. He had to get across the road now for his pre-dinner drink. Two dollars for a decent chardonnay. Did I play pool? They'd just put in a pool table. 'I'd play sooner rather than later if I were you. The velvet is already taking a hammering.'

I said I didn't play.

'Do you swim?' asked Mr Wilson.

'A bit in summer.'

'You'd have a tremendous advantage. Look at your wingspan! I swim every morning. Nice wee lap pool. Get there at the right time and you have it to yourself.' He pointed at my phone. 'Do you have enough? Can't imagine it's of any interest really.'

'No, it'll be good. Thank you, Mr Wilson. I'll listen and make some notes. But overall you're going to be a great addition to the human library.'

He laughed at this. 'Oh, and hopefully it won't have recorded too much of your snoring.' He winked at me as I was leaving.

Had I really been snoring? Was this just his little joke or had he truly rumbled me? I biked along Pleasant Lane, a ghost sword in my hand, aimed at the letterboxes. The blossoms were scrappy now, appearing only on the odd branch of each tree, and the piles of fallen blossoms were rusty and damp. My front wheel ploughed through them, hardly registering the effort.

As he waded out into the lake and the cool water reached his thighs, then his middle, he ran his fingers across the surface, making small circles. He could see the sandy bottom, lit by a sudden arrow of tiny luminous fish. When he dipped his head and swam underneath the surface, the fish scattered. Soon it was too deep to see the bottom. Murky shapes of plant life appeared. He pushed on. Then he stopped, treading water and looking around. The shore was farther away than he'd expected and he felt a moment of panic. Could he make it back if he cramped up? The water was colder out here. He was a very average swimmer, untested really. Yet he was out in the middle of the lake. Still, he owed it to his friend to look for him. Everyone else had given up. But he wouldn't give up.

Then a surprise. Another one. That night Mr Wilson phoned. He apologised for the call. Was it convenient now to talk? Because he'd been speaking to his daughter that same evening and she was a bit annoyed at him. He'd told her about the human library project and she'd asked if he'd come up with something about the earthquakes. No, he told her. Why not? Because, he said, I won't be the hundredth or thousandth person to talk about events that came out of the blue and really had nothing to do with my life except they happened to me by chance. And she was peeved. She told me I was being silly. She said I could tell whatever story I wanted but there was no reason to rule out the earthquakes. You see my wife, my daughter's mother, was badly affected by those random events. She saw a person die on the street when all she'd done was go into Cashel Street Mall for some shopping. Meaning the person who died and my wife, both of them had the same purpose but one of them died and one of them witnessed it. And this upset my wife a great deal and affected her for years in many ways.

Was his wife still alive? Probably not. Unless she was locked up somewhere. I hadn't thought to ask when I was doing the recording session.

'I'm sorry to be giving you these details now, Ricky, and over the phone. I'm an engineer, that was my training and that's my excuse. My wife often said when I spoke in a slightly unusual way, oh, don't mind him, he's an engineer. I know our reputation. It's fine. The world needs people of all sorts, even the sort I am. And I said to my daughter I wouldn't be telling you or anyone else this story since it was too private. I explained to her that this was for your school project and I wouldn't be asking a fifteen-year-old boy—sorry Ricky—to offer me editing tips on the story of the moment which profoundly disturbed the shape of my wife's life. And yes, I have returned not too long ago from that pool table I spoke of, having enjoyed some two-dollar treats, not sure how many, and I must report that the tip of my pool cue did pass at an odd angle while delivering a glancing blow to the white ball and ending up causing a small rip in the velvet. I'll pay. I'll pay. No, I won't be saddling you with all of that sorry business from Cashel Street Mall, Ricky. However, there's this. Can I give you this?'

'Please,' I said.

'While my wife was in town shopping, I was at the QEII memorial pool. I do love my swimming, as I told you. The quake hit when I was just getting out of the water. At first I thought oh, must have got out too quickly. My balance was off. Take a moment. Steady yourself. Blood will return to the right places. I have low blood pressure. But there was no steadying. I looked up then at the ceiling, which was moving. And the noise! Then the water in the pool rose. The lane ropes disappeared. The water went hurtling to one end, flooding over the sides, washing chairs and a few people who'd been standing by the side of the pool into the water. I remember gripping something, maybe a locker door that had been flung open. I ended up with a small cut on my hand somehow. Then the wave of water was sucked back in the opposite direction and I saw it rise as if we were in a huge storm at sea, right up and over the ladder leading up to the lifeguard's station. The young chap up there, I saw his face and it was pure terror. But as the water took his seat from under him, he dived clear. He went under the wave. I lost him. He was hurled inside the pool's vortex. People were screaming. I myself was probably shouting. I know I was. Not a clue what I said. Something like, "No! No! Stop this right now!" The lights had gone out. Daylight still came through the windows but it was suddenly very dim inside, like we were in a plane passing through dark clouds. Then the lifeguard reappeared right across the far side of the pool, bodysurfing, I suppose you'd call it, until the water receded and he found himself on the tiles of the floor, moving his arms and legs. A starfish! He stood up and walked towards some swimmers who were also now getting to their knees, looking around. What just happened? What just happened? And I looked into the QEII pool and the water had vanished! A few puddles had formed near huge cracks. But the water was gone.'

Mr Wilson was silent for a moment. What to say to him? 'I—'

'Perhaps,' he said, 'I could make this my book. I'd like to offer this, Ricky. For my daughter and my wife. Do you think? Not too upsetting? No one was seriously hurt. It was a … startlement. Not a word. I'll find a better word. Who was that lifeguard? He was hardly older than you. Who was the young girl I met who told me she would run home now? She was your age. She was still in her togs. She would run home to check on her mother

134

and brother. Her father normally picked her up from the pool but not until later. How far is it? I asked her. How far is home? Not far, she said. Five kilometres or something. She would be okay running home. And off she went, leaping over the liquefaction in her bare feet and togs.'

The text version of the above I sent to Keri was a mess. Halfway through, something clicked: Oh, she's from Auckland and doesn't have a point of reference for either Christchurch or earthquakes. I may as well have been saying South Sudan and civil war. She texted: Poor guy sounds cracked. But that wasn't true, was it? I didn't know how to answer that. I wanted to defend him. Then she texted: I asked Dad who Le Clair is.

I texted: WHO IS HE??????

> business associate
> that's it?? how/when/where etc?
> mumbled something about food business being full of oddballs
> covering up something?
> maybe but he always seems like he's covering up something even when he's not ya know?
> yeah
> anywayzzzz changing da subject. soz eh
> for what soz?
> you making me say it out loud?
> text out loud
> saturday. the forest. that was a PB in shitness
> all sweet
> you didn't text till now

> you neither
>
> snap!
>
> sorry here from me to youse too
>
> wass your crime?
>
> unloading ma shit
>
> this is a thing we share our shit yeah?
>
> cool
>
> you make aspiring fucked up
>
> in good way?
>
> interesting way. good is too hard to say right now.
>
> jury out dot dot dot
>
> agree 1000%

No texts for a while. I put down my phone and walked around my room. Looked at the poster of the arch. Touched poster, got nothing from it. Picked up phone. It was hot, overheating. Battery problem? Would it burst into flames? I reread all the messages from Keri. Then I asked:

> how come you believe in god? small g or big G??
>
> state pref

Long pause. Put down phone again. Zilch. Maybe I'd offended her. It was the wrong question, was it? People believe stuff. It's their right. But Keri didn't seem like the offendable type. Thoughts of leaving my room, getting something to eat from the kitchen. Straightened my basketball boots beside my chest of drawers. Third pair in six months and even these newish ones were starting to cramp my toes.

Ping!

> not fussed g/G
>
> good to get that sorted. soz for stupid question
>
> I'm only naming a mystery with the g word.
>
> not bossing anyone or anything

do you pray? (he asked pryingly)

I have some talking I do

Jesus, was I praying too then? Were my looping sentences addressed to Someone Else. But I'd had no religion in my life and, to be honest, hadn't missed it. Did she go to church?

go to church?

I LIKE churches

explain?

they smell nice. shouldn't you be getting your
beauty sleep ahead of THE GAME?

after mikey died mum started praying

you need to be careful

careful of what?

people

16.

Minivans are hell for tall people. All vehicles pretty much. By what means are the Golden State Warriors transported to and fro? Steven Adams on sixty mill, I still feel your pain, bro.

The ride to Dunedin was finally over. We were at the home of the Southern Dunks, about to dunk on them. I unfolded myself into the overcast coolness of the stadium carpark. We were going straight into a training session before checking in to the motel ahead of the play-off that night.

He found his father running around the garage, frantically opening the doors of the cars he was servicing. What's wrong? he asked. Oh, my God, his father said, it's the pollinators! The what? he said. The pollinators, the pollinators! I can't find the pollinators. I think someone's stolen them! But Dad, he said, cars don't have pollinators. The earth has pollinators, not cars. His father gripped his arm. But where are they?'

Coach Dennett was using a different tactic. No barking, no jibes, no humiliation. Suddenly we were adults on a shared mission of solemn importance. In the changing rooms he came to each of us in turn for a quiet chat, inquiring about our well-being, whatever niggles we were carrying, our week leading up to this day, our families. Finally he named the quality he saw in us that set us apart. I could hear some of these private pronouncements. Bravery. Positivity. For you, it's curiosity. For you, stamina. A sense of adventure. But in addition to this known quality, he was saying, we each had something else, something deep down that we'd never really uncovered or admitted. I couldn't hear what these were because he leaned in close to announce them. Quietly he was suggesting how each of us could become a new thing, a fuller individual. 'Ricky,' he said softly, sitting beside me as I laced my shoes, 'for you the most shining quality, the obvious thing, is loyalty. Do I have that right?'

I nodded.

'You always look out for your friends. You put others first.'

Nod here.

'No one else in this team has undergone a more dramatic change than you in such a short time. Yet through that period, you've stayed the same in yourself. Loyal.'

Immediately this seemed a failing. He meant I hadn't improved a jot, loyalty was my gift, my curse. I was stuck at this point. Forever loyal. *Call me loyal. Keeeep it that way.*

Coach looked at the floor. Our knees were almost touching. Most of the other players had left the changing room. We heard their shouts from the court.

'I think now you can add something to this wonderful gift of loyalty.' He looked at me. 'You have it in you, I know you do. Ownership.'

'Ownership,' I said.

'Do you think?'

I nodded.

'Good.' He gave my knee a bump with his fist. 'Good, Ricky.' He stood up and clapped his hands, looking around the empty room. As he walked out, he bent down and set a drink bottle upright from where it had fallen on its side.

At the motel I was sharing a unit with Sim, Johnny, and Angus. Johnny always threw up before a game, no matter the stakes. But the play-off had turned his insides to concrete. His bowels hadn't moved for two days. 'You guys don't want to be around when the dam bursts,' he said.

Sim was also backed-up, but verbally. He seemed to be living behind his eyes.

'You good, Sim?' I asked.

He lifted his eyebows in assent.

Johnny said, 'He's like an opera singer whispering before a big performance. Saving himself.'

Angus came out of the toilet.

'Here's a man who's not saving himself,' said Johnny. 'Would you close the door, big Angus beef?'

Angus went to the fridge and looked inside. He'd done it several times already. It was empty apart from two little cartons of milk.

'Do you think it's a magic fridge?' said Johnny. 'Between the last time you looked and this time, it'll produce a sandwich?'

'Coach said my quality was hope,' said Angus.

'What did he want you to add to it?' I said.

Angus closed the fridge door and looked at the ceiling. 'Shit, I forget.'

'Maybe it was reality,' said Johnny.

'Nup,' said Angus.

We were waiting for our dinner. Pizzas. Johnny left to go for a walk around the block, to see if things would loosen. Angus turned on the television again, went through all the channels, and turned it off. Sim moved wordlessly into the bedroom he was sharing with Johnny.

Angus sat down on the sofa opposite my chair. 'I hear you want my crown.'

'Eh?' I said.

'You were seen. With the girl from Pete's.'

'Was I?'

'Yeah.' He was grinning at me. 'Biking as fast as you could. Was what I heard.'

'Really?'

'Uh-huh. So do I have to pass on my crown or not, Ricky?'

I shook my head. 'You're still the king.'

He slapped the arm of the sofa. 'Okay! But I feel my reign is threatened. Who is she, that girl? You're mixed up in something, Ricky, and I don't understand it. That's cool, bro. That's cool.'

Whenever I'd thought of the play-off before stepping on court, it was always in slow motion, a series of errors or good things but always patterns of play I could see and reflect on, adjust to, inhabit or reject as needed. Imagining it, I was aware of playing the game as I was playing it. It came with time and thought. Yes, I see. Okay, now this is happening. I will do this. What a fantasy!

After the actual tip-off, the thing was a complete blur. Bodies, voices, whistles. It was more like being punched. Like being back in the shoe store with those thugs. Ooof. Punched. Then kicked. Then punched again before I had time to say to myself, oh, that was a punch, better do something different next time. The next time was piled on top of this time and this time and this time. Not even the hammering we took from the senior team in that warm-up game was preparation for this. The seniors had visited violence on us. But this was better—I mean worse—in that I found myself in the middle of the pleasurable feeling—believe me!—of being done like a dinner, stitched up, hung out to dry.

The Southern Dunks were very good. Everything was faster. Occasionally something would happen involving me that did in fact work out. But I couldn't build anything from the experience. It was gone in a puff. My puff, my puffing. Sometimes I had the feeling I was being made to play for the opposing team. They were engineering it so I was a positive on-court influence for them!

At quarter-time, Coach Dennett, the real one, was back.

'Do people want to go back to the motel now? Is that it? Is there something on TV you're missing? Shall I start chucking the gear in the van? Huh?'

'No, Coach,' said Johnny.

'No? Anyone else want to play alongside this guy?'

'Yes, Coach,' said Angus.

Then we all joined in. Yes, Coach. We wanna play! Yes!

Bench me, I pleaded. *Bench me, you idiot!* Why wasn't I getting the evil eye? Could it be true they were all experiencing the game in the same way I was? That the storm wasn't just in my head? I looked into the faces of my team-mates. Yes, general shock. Except Johnny. He ran from our huddle in the direction of the toilets.

Sim took hold of my elbow. He looked possessed, manic. 'Their number four,' he told me, speaking right in my ear, 'you stand in front of him. You stand on top of him. You play in his fucking shoes! You're not his shadow, you're him! He hasn't got legs any more because you're wearing them, got it?'

He had his voice back.

'Sure, Sim,' I said. 'Then I get fouled out.'

'Who cares! In the time it takes for you to draw five fouls, at least he won't have scored his usual allotment of a billion fucking three-pointers. Snuffle him, stamp on him, choke the fucker. Understand?'

'I'll try.'

He tugged harder at my elbow. '*Own* him!'

Johnny raced onto court just in time. If he'd had shit running down his leg, we wouldn't have been surprised. As it was, Johnny's face was filled with a new kind of fever and heat. His arms were loose and his hips were mobile again. He grabbed an intercept almost at once, dribbled the length of the court, and laid it off with a no-look pass for an easy bucket. He was a demon fresh from the furnace where they forge demons and rats. And basketballers.

I walked into their number four.

He gave me a shove.

I leaned across him full-body style.

He was 6'5". 'Hey, droopy,' he said, spitting into my ear. 'How come you're not benched?'

I spun with my elbow wearing his ribs.

From the floor, skidding on his arse, he waved his arms. 'You see that, ref? See that?'

Coach Dennett was out of his seat, telling the kid to get up, get up, stop milking it! The ref looked between the kid and the coach and gave it to the coach.

I rode his instep when he tried to jump. I caught his chin with my shoulder when I jumped, though the ball was nowhere.

From the polished floor he was yelling again.

Their coach won this time. Foul!

Away from all this, Angus was muscling inside, bucket after bucket. Johnny was finding Sim, who popped in consecutive three-pointers, one from each side, then a third from the middle. Their man marking failed to adjust. Timeout!

We were ahead by six. Nothing, a lead like that. But still.

Coach Dennett said to us, 'They're switching to zone defence. Understand? We know what to do. We made them switch. So now we know what to do.'

And somehow we did. Even I knew. Sort of. I just followed Sim's orders and mashed into their number four as often as I could. I was fouled out just before half-time and Coach Dennett slapped me on the back and said, 'You put in a shift, Clemens!'

In the fury of playing, I can't say I took in the crowd. They were there as the backboards were there, as the scoreboard was there, as the floor was and the lights in the ceiling. People? Yes, of course they'd be part of a play-off game. Some parents had travelled with us. The bulk of the crowd was made up of rival supporters since they lived closer to the neutral venue. We'd never played in front of this many people but that didn't really register. Not as pressure. Ludicrous as it seems, I had a tiny intimation of what it would be like to play in front of forty thousand or four hundred thousand. The numbers got bigger but the size of your feelings stayed the same. It was only when I sat down and became one of them, one of the watching crowd, that my nerves kicked in and my stomach tightened and my notion of the sheer significance of this particular moment changed to *fuckmefuckmefuckmewhatifwelosewhatifwewinfuck.*

I seemed to care suddenly. Loyalty? Not sure. I was shouting myself hoarse anyway.

The Dunks went ahead late in the third quarter. Johnny had hurt his knee in a scrap for a loose ball. He played on but without the same zing or step. Angus went cold under the hoop. Their best player started popping them in. For the first time I saw a look on Coach Dennett's face. Not resignation but a brief flash of 'this is slipping away from us'. He'd stopped scribbling in his notebook and had started stalking the sideline, glaring at players, ours and theirs as if he couldn't tell the difference any more. As if both teams were conspiring to ruin his night, ruin his season, ruin his life.

Oh, and Mr Le Clair was taking it all in from the top row.

I'd spotted him late in the quarter when I'd glanced up at a group of boys who were chanting for the opposition. So maybe he lived in Dunedin and just liked basketball and had a free Tuesday.

Or he was here to see me.

He was my scout! Not for basketball, hell no.

Then what?

In the break we looked a bit lost. There was less planning talk, more creeping blame, a few accusations. Johnny said he wondered if anyone else wanted to join him on the forward press because it was getting a little lonely. Someone else mumbled something about Johnny's gammy knee and a walking stick. Coach Dennett squashed that one but there were other mini fires of recrimination and sliding confidence. With time called, Sim said, 'Angus, bro, what's happening? You shot your wad already? Get your head out of the fucking forest!' Angus lunged for Sim and had to be held back.

Before I took my seat again I glanced up at Le Clair. He was gone.

Against predictions and common sense, we actually started the final quarter well, helped no doubt by their best player rolling his ankle on his first drive to the line. We hadn't laid a hand on him but there he was, a heap of pain in a skid of sweat, prone at our feet. It was as though the gods had struck him down. And it gave us a boost. Fluidity came back into our passing game. Angus went up at the end of a great full-court move and dunked it tremendously. How did he get up that high? Chest pumps all round. On the bench as well. Our parents rose and cheered, the loudest sound of the evening so far.

We tied them and then the lead bounced between us, never more than a couple of buckets in it.

They called a timeout with possession and eight seconds left. We were ahead by three points. Calm now ruled in our camp, or at least a simulation of calm. Coach Dennett spoke clearly, without panic, showing the boys on his whiteboard, with a few neat strokes, the next and final defensive play. The boys looked steadily at the circles and lines, nodding. Coach's black marker pen had conjured their forms perfectly. Yes, I *am* that circle and I *shall* move in that direction while the other circles move around me. Here was the last dance.

Shut down the middle and make them go wide. Hassle, hassle, no fouls. We step in and foul the ball-carrier at four seconds, five seconds max. That would take them to the free-throw line for two. There'd be one more timeout. We organise again at that point.

What happened next? What the hell happened?

The drive home early the next morning was at first a matter of looking out the windows of the van, trying to see something in the pre-dawn blackness, something other than your own reflected face or the faces of your team-mates. All of us put on headphones, even Coach. Why did we have to check out so early, posting our room keys through the after-hours slot? But we supposed that had a rightness, to sneak away under cover of darkness. And this despite the nice post-game speech from the parents about how proud they were of us and how proud we should be of ourselves for getting to this stage of the season for the first time ever. The Dunks captain had said nice words, too, and their coach. Our coach found it harder to be positive. Clearly he had no sense of the long view yet. The wounds were raw. He was like us, hoping to crawl off somewhere.

He sat up front next to the driver, oversized headphones looking like he was the co-pilot on some astral mission, staring straight ahead into Otago nothing.

Then the objects of the hiding world slowly took shape: the roadside grass, the fences and sheep, the cows and hills, the crops, the trucks. A tractor far-off on a hillside stayed in view for several long minutes. He didn't give a shit about basketball and nor did we. Climate change didn't give a shit about basketball and nor did we! My long-dead brother didn't give a shit. Nor did I.

Flashes of the high stone embankments of the Clutha River as it cut through paddocks. Vineyards.

It took a while before the first post-mortems kicked in. We had a toilet stop at Cromwell and when we got back in the van, something had shifted. We wondered aloud: Who'd not covered the pass that went forty metres to be plucked under the hoop by one of their forwards? Then who'd not covered this next bit? That instead of the easy bucket poked in from underneath, the ball had travelled back out beyond the circle to a player, also free—who was supposed to be on him?—and nothing-but-net in went the three-pointer to tie it. Four seconds left. And who saw this next horror coming? That they didn't call a timeout and nor did we. Coach, are you listening? Coach? And instead of protecting possession, we forgot the percentages. All they did was snaffle a loose ball—how did that happen?—and waltz it down court for a regulation lay-up until—fucking *finally*—Sim stepped into the guy's path, downing him. One second left on the clock. Guy slots his first free throw crowd goes ape good night nurse where's the minivan.

In the motel room I'd slept like a baby, like a concussed baby. The bottle of vodka Angus had brought remained unopened. In the other rooms the older guys had drunk a beer or two, then crashed out. There was a bag of weed rumoured to be available in room thirty-two. Sim had been going on about it before the game, how we were going to be lit like Christmas trees. But he never went and knocked on that door. We'd all gone to bed early.

And now we'd woken.

It seemed our failure could rightly be shared among us. No one got off in the rundown of mistakes. Those of us on the pine when the shit went down were also hauled in, rightly. What had we done to assist the cause? Zilch and zero and nada respectively.

I prodded Sim, who was sitting beside me. He took off his headphones. 'You know who was there at the game? Mr Le Clair.'

'Who?'

'Dude who comes to the restaurant.'

'I don't wanna talk about that right now.' He put his headphones on again.

In the front of the van, Johnny and a couple of others were still arguing, though the urgency had gone out of it now that a single culprit could not be located. I put my headphones back on. Frank Ocean, speak to me.

Ten minutes later Sim bumped my elbow, wanting to talk. 'Why was he there? Why was that guy at our basketball game?'

'No idea,' I said. 'What's been happening with your stepbrother's goons and the shoe store?'

'They paid a visit again. Business as normal.'

'Bugger.' I felt bad for not following up on this earlier. The Keri stuff had swallowed things.

'They're okay. No one got hurt this time. Bruiser Clemens wasn't around. Hey, you did the deal on their number four, eh.'

'I can put it about, yeah.'

Sim laughed. 'I'm not sure I know you any more.'

'Me neither.'

Then he wanted to know about the girl I'd been seen with. I told him about Pete's, her waitressing job, the climbing wall, the Saturday bike ride. I managed to give him plenty of details but none of—what? The truth? But what was the truth? Me afraid? Auntie Rena turning up at that terrible family dinner and making us cry with a song?

I tried to think of a cartoon we could share. Nothing came. *Put away childish things.*

The van came over the last rise into Aspiring township and there was the lake. Strange to be surprised by a body of water you've spent your whole life next to. Did you think it was going somewhere? But that was what I felt, as if I'd met someone I wasn't expecting, a friend I hadn't seen in ages and who shouldn't really be in this position, right in front of my eyes. You! How?

The lake had a satiny molten finish. The little island in its middle, so often a bushy smudge, was sharply defined, its trees upright and piercing. Towering behind, the group of snow-capped peaks appeared closer than normal. It was as if an HD camera had zoomed in on the whole landscape. Soon the mountaineers moving up the slopes of Mount Aspiring, Tititea, would change from invisible to dots to human figures with faces. One of them would have my face. The world was ending, the houses of the super-rich were smoking ruins, and I was climbing over the Southern Alps, sliding down the retreating glaciers to reach the Tasman Sea, gateway to …

When the van pulled in by the lakefront stop, Coach Dennett finally turned to us. He asked that the door not be opened yet since he had a few things to say to us. 'You'll all be thinking about the game, I know, I know. That was tough last night.' Then he was telling us about our achievements and how well we'd done and how we could hold our heads up high. He'd worked up enough internal strength to deliver the speech he couldn't deliver after the game.

But it struck me that I wasn't thinking about the game any more. I was thinking: this is where she is! Keri is here. I was wondering about the shape of her feet, their feel in my hands. And: did I figure in her prayers? Dear God, whoever you are.

Yet walking home above the lake, my mind went back to the game again. Le Clair. Had he left once I'd fouled out? Had he really come to see me play?

I felt a coolness nip at my ankles and, looking down, I saw my jeans were now a little bit shorter than they had been. It was like being bitten by a small invisible dog.

17.

Keri arrived for her shift just as I was taking a bag of rubbish to the bins outside. I'd texted her earlier about the play-off game and she'd texted back a crying face. Good, I thought at first, she's sad for me. But what had happened to her no-emojis rule? Maybe she was only ironically sad. Or did she mean *I* was crying and she knew it? Or perhaps she meant I *should* be crying since that was what a feeling person did on these occasions? Or I *shouldn't* be crying because it was only a stupid game, hence stupid emoji?

All of this was probably my fault. I'd given her no clear read on my attitude to the sport or on our chance to make history. Confusion reigned. Best to emoji back and leave all the doubt in place. In person, she rushed and hugged me. Oh! For a second I almost burst into tears. When we stepped apart, she reached up and shoved me in the chest, laughing. 'Loser!'

'Thanks a lot!' I said. She'd rescued me. I flipped the rubbish bag into the bin and followed her through the back door of Pete's.

Both Mum and Dad had been at work when I made it home that morning. Mum had called me the previous night to hear how the game had gone. We'd talked for a few minutes. Had I eaten a proper dinner? Was the motel warm enough? Then she put Dad on. 'Ah, well,' he said immediately, 'you did your best.' But I hadn't said anything yet about how I'd performed. Then he said, 'You'll be keeping your chins up.' He was on automatic pilot. 'There was a kid on TV last night. He was twelve years old and seven foot. Canada, I think. They had to play him in the junior league, where he didn't have to leave the ground to dunk the ball. Ludicrous!'

I ended up grunting in agreement with every inane thing he said. Finally I said I had to go because we had a team meeting.

There was a pause and Dad said, 'When we didn't hear straight away from you, your mother thought you'd probably lost. But I said to her maybe they've won and he's too caught up in the celebrations to call. That gave us both a bit of hope.'

His voice was suddenly different.

'Sorry,' I said. 'It was just difficult to call.'

'Or text,' he said.

'Yeah, sorry. We had to hand in our phones before the game. Coach's rule. Then it was all a bit …'

'Right. Anyway, I'd like to hear about it properly when you get back. It's a real achievement what you've done.' He seemed on the brink of saying something more. Something about Mikey, I thought with a sinking heart. Just for once, could it not be about Mikey? Mikey had also been to Dunedin on a sporting trip. Had never come back. Was this the something more Dad was on the cusp of saying? Had they both been terrified I wouldn't come back? I hadn't given them a thought. And I hadn't thought of my little big bro the entire trip. Suddenly I felt crushed, squashed. Felt bad for Mikey, bad for my folks. But the words didn't come and we said goodbye.

Garth found me in the back room, standing against his height chart. 'Self-measuring?' he said.

I stepped away from the wall, leaving my hand where the top of my head had been. It was half an inch or so above the last mark. Garth peered up at it and shook his head.

'Now you don't have to lose money to Mr Le Clair,' I said.

He stared at me. 'We're stopping all that. It's unhealthy.' He wet his finger with his tongue and tried to rub at the ladder of marks on the wall above the chart. He rubbed harder but the marks didn't come off. He looked around for another means, a cloth?

'You'll leave Keri's though?' I said. Suddenly that seemed important. I wouldn't let him take down the chart with Keri's marks. Her history was written there.

'No, no. It's all gotta go. I'll get the whole room repainted. It's overdue.' Without bothering to remove the drawing pins, Garth tugged at the height chart, tearing it from its place, revealing a whiter shape on the wall. 'Bloody grubby in here,' he said.

'Can I have it?' I said.

'What? The chart? No. Why'd you want it?' He scanned the room with its piles of papers on his wonky desk, the filing cabinet whose bottom drawer wouldn't close properly, old pieces of kitchen equipment stacked badly in the far corner. He folded up the chart roughly and stuffed it behind a cardboard box. 'Ricky, sit down a minute. My neck's getting sore. Sit. Sit!' I perched on the stool that only he had rights to while Garth stood. 'Probably this is terrible timing with the basketball loss just hitting, but you might have noticed we're not exactly thriving here in the restaurant business.'

Ah, Jesus, I felt it coming. 'I think it's your social media,

Garth,' I said. 'I think it's your brand.' Did he ever read those TripAdvisor burns?

He scratched his ear. 'I had the accountant in the other day. Those bastards don't muck around. They hit you with figures. They do the sums. They say things like, "the numbers don't lie". They are very depressing people. Anyway, the accountant made me a cost-cutting plan.'

'Take some things off the menu that aren't popular,' I said. I'd watched *Save My Restaurant* on TV.

'Staff costs are the first item on these bastards' agendas. Upshot is I can't afford you any more, Ricky.'

There was a sharp whoosh in my ears. 'I can't work here any more?' I said.

'The numbers don't lie.'

'What if I took a pay cut?'

'Ha! Well, we'd be breaking the law. But no, Ricky. Sorry, boss.'

'What about Mr Le Clair?'

'What about him?'

'He . . . won't he?' *Miss me? Ask for me? Require me?*

'Won't he what?' said Garth.

'He was at the play-off game! He was in Dunedin, watching us play.'

'Yeah, his son plays. He was in the opposition team. Le Clair didn't want to bring it up with you. Didn't want to get in your head.'

'He has a son?'

'Rory? Roly? Rory, I think.'

'Rory?'

'Pretty good player by all accounts. Did you talk to Mr Le Clair?'

'He was only there for part of the game. He left. He left when I was fouled out.'

'Huh. But he's never anywhere for long. He's always walking out on me.'

'What does he do?'

'What does he do? You mean for a living? I haven't a clue. He does deals. I don't know half of what he does. One thing is he tries to hook up inventors with capital. The sawn-off Caddy he gets around in—that's something from a while back. Prototype eco-vehicle type thing. Thought he could change the way people, especially Americans, thought about cars. Ahead of his time probably. Never went anywhere that particular venture. But he ends up with the weird car.'

'How come he hangs out here?'

'A long time ago we met at a thing.'

'What thing?'

'Okay, it was like a men's group.'

'A men's group?'

'For men who—why am I telling you this? For men who'd lost their wives.'

'Oh.' I didn't want to hear about this group. 'You lost your wife … in Auckland?'

'That was my second wife, Keri's mother. My first wife died. Long time ago.'

I didn't want to hear about his first wife. My head was spinning. I was getting the sack. 'Mr Le Clair wears a pin, a badge. It's the Gateway Arch in St Louis, Missouri.'

'Is that what it is?'

'Why wear that?'

'Was he from there originally? Somewhere in the States anyway, I never asked. But he's lived in New Zealand a long time and he's never going back. Why do you want to know about Le Clair?'

'I don't know. He's a mystery.'

'Jesus, we're all mysteries, Ricky.'

'Really?'

'All of us.' He reached over to me, holding out his hand. 'Even me. Even you.' It took me a few moments to realise what he was doing. He wanted to shake my hand! Goodbye and good luck. I'd never seen Garth shake anyone's hand. Garth shook fists not hands.

When my shift ended—my final shift—Keri was serving and I couldn't face her anyway. I said goodbye to Logan and Dave. They hugged me and said see you around big fella.

Biking home, the wind off the lake whipped at my eyes. I felt tears leaking and drying almost at once. Was that the order: wind then tears? Probably not.

It struck me too that I hadn't had a loop in my head since the play-off game. The silence was not total, however. I had an awareness of silence as if I'd entered a cavernous empty building and the door had closed behind me. No sentence came to me that went: *If only I could find the door again, I could make it outside and search for the missing members of my family.* Nope. I was simply aware of a space. I was afraid. I was afraid of myself. People looked at me, unable to tell my age. Big deal. I looked at myself, unable to tell anything.

When I got home I took down my poster of the St Louis arch, rolling it up and storing it at the back of my wardrobe. It left a large blank space. I almost unrolled the poster to stick it back up again. I looked at my basketball boots and put them in the wardrobe as well. I looked at the books on my shelves, things from when I was twelve, thirteen, fourteen. I looked at my duvet cover: blue boats? Who'd bought that? I looked at my lampshade:

a pirate motif? Who had placed these Lord of the Rings figurines on my windowsill? Who had been in here while I was away?

A text from Keri: meet tomorrow after school?

My hand was shaking.

    yes where?

    sf

    sure?

    bring provisions

18.

We were invited up on stage at senior assembly. The principal, Mr Jamieson (5'11"), called us 'outstanding'. He said our narrow loss had brought credit to the whole school and showed that the future was bright for basketball in the region. He said that the new stadium being built by the new primary school and the new supermarket and the new artificial hockey pitches would further encourage the development of such fine talent. I could barely follow what he was saying. 'Please join me in congratulating the entire team!' Loud applause and whistling came from the hall. Then we filed past and Coach Dennett shook our hands as our names were read out.

When Johnny walked across the stage, someone called out, 'Stand up, Stockton!' and Johnny mimed walking down an invisible set of stairs, getting lower and lower to the floor. The whole audience laughed, even most of the teachers. Next it was Angus, who came across the stage with one hand in his pocket. The shout went out: 'Achieved! Achieved! Achieved!'

I walked across to polite applause. And just as I was at the edge of the stage, a lone voice I couldn't identify called out 'Sticky'. There was some murmuring but it was lost in the announcement of the next name.

In English we talked about the human library. I had my two books, though I had no idea which story they'd tell or whether they'd tell the right ones. When I concentrated and listened to the outlines of some of my classmates' books, I saw potential issues with both Miss Milton and Mr Wilson if they went the death-haunted way. The other human books were upbeat, amusing, hopeful, warming. A missing hunting dog that turned up after a year. A funny fishing trip. Hiking in the Himalayas. Solo sailing around the world. Founding a charity. Lifelong learning. It appeared there were very few yarns about the brain surgery of a potential murderer or girls running home in their togs through liquefaction.

Miss Clarke said she was really interested in Kathy Wang's book. There were such rich stories waiting to be told that had never been told before.

Kathy said, 'My book is Mrs Petrie. She coaches tennis.'

'Oh,' said Miss Clarke, disappointed. 'She has one arm.'

'Yeah, she's a really good coach.'

'Did none of your family want to take part, Kathy?'

Kathy spoke quietly, 'I thought Mrs Petrie was better.'

Miss Clarke blinked hard. 'Oh, no,' she said. 'No, no, no, Kathy. No one is better than anyone else for the human library.'

'But,' said Kathy slowly, 'you think someone from my family is better than Mrs Petrie?'

'Because they're Chinese,' someone said from the back of the class.

'No,' said Miss Clarke. 'You've made a fine choice, Kathy. Very good.'

I fudged the report on my two books, speaking vaguely about senior citizens. Anyway, the focus was on those of us who didn't have anyone lined up. Angus. Could someone perhaps help Angus find a book?

I had an old rug in my backpack and a small cushion. A cool wind had come up again, stripping the last of the blossoms off the trees by the lake. Biking past the playground, I checked my phone. Two texts from Keri. Too cold, said the first one. Then: Come to mine. Garth at work.

I'd never been to Garth's house before. Some people, you don't imagine them actually living anywhere. You can't picture them having a bedroom they sleep in, a bathroom with a bath mat they have to wash, a study with a drawer full of adapters and USB cables. Garth was like that, I realised. He was so strongly part of the restaurant, I guess I'd always seen him living out his life there, among knives, pots, customers, heat, and grease.

It turned out he lived in the old part of Aspiring, on the rise above the eastern side of the lake in a street of small single-storey houses looked over by a new development of larger houses built for the view. And you just knew developers were waiting for the orginal owners of places like Garth's to drop off their perches so that premium properties could be built. More than once my dad had pointed to stories in the paper about elderly residents turning down a million dollars, more. 'They think everyone has a price. But some people have values other than money.'

'Still,' Mum said, 'a million dollars is a lot of money for not much house. I'd be tempted.'

'And you'd resist temptation,' said Dad.

'Would I?'

The strangest thing about Garth's abode—and it was very abodey—was not the neatness of the front garden, with its trimmed hedge and flower beds, or the stone path with its pointless turns like the turns in a line at an airport—I remembered LAX from our US trip—and not even the carved wooden Home Sweet Home plaque on the front door. The strangest thing was the Smurfs.

When Keri opened the door, I saw them lined up on a high ledge that ran around the walls of the hallway. Further inside, they were everywhere. Where books might have been, there were shelved Smurfs. In the living room there was a large cabinet with glass doors and it was full of Smurfs. Where cups and crockery might have been, there were kitchen Smurfs.

'What?' said Keri. 'Doesn't *your* father have a hobby?'

I remembered the time a petrol station was giving Smurfs away as a promotion and I'd got a few. 'I was hoping they were yours,' I said.

'You mean you were hoping they weren't mine.'

'How many has he got?'

'Everyone asks that.'

Stranger still, I felt my nerves relax a little under the gaze of all these figurines. Papa Smurf. Pretentious Smurf. Harmony Smurf with his trumpet. Painter Smurf with his easel. Approaching the house, I wasn't breathing right. I was sweaty. I could have easily turned away, texted some excuse. Scaredy Smurf. But tough old Garth loved *these* things? Not just loved them but needed them always in view? It calmed me down. Chillin' Smurf.

We were standing in the kitchen, and grouped by the stove were the various cooking Smurfs in their chef's hats, their baker's aprons. How odd that Pete's was Smurf-free. But I supposed these were Garth's special collection. They made sense together. No point in scattering a few here and there. This was where they lived happily in their community.

Keri's bedroom was the only place in the house that didn't have Smurfs.

It had almost nothing in it. A full-length mirror. A chest of drawers above which hung a painting of the lake. A large half-filled suitcase in the corner, spilling clothes. A chair with more clothes thrown on it. On an otherwise bare shelving unit beside the double bed, a few toiletries. It was like a motel room whose occupant would be checking out in the morning. There was not a touch of childhood. No teddy bears, no girly posters, no photo boards. Maybe the room had never been Keri's room.

Keri was in bare feet. 'Take off your shoes,' she said.

'Shall I leave my socks on?' I said.

'I'm not going to tell you everything you have to do, am I?' She'd spoken harshly but now she smiled. She was joking. I hadn't picked that up immediately and she saw it. My nerves were back. I needed a Smurf or two in my eye line.

We sat down on the edge of the bed.

She glanced at me, then back at the carpet. 'I don't go around sleeping with under-age boys, you know. It's illegal.'

'What if I consented?' I said.

'I don't think that's usually how consent works.'

We sat in silence.

'Hey, Mopey Smurf,' she said.

'Is that one of them?'

'I have no fucking idea.' She stared up at me. 'Um, you have to meet me at my level, eh.' She gestured that I tip my head down and then she moved her head up and we were kissing. Whatever pain I had in my jaw from basketball was gone. When we stopped she asked me to close the curtains. In the moment I did that, she had taken off her top and crossed her arms over her chest. She was wearing a black bra.

'Okay, okay,' she said, 'so these are hardly winning prizes.'

Again it took me a moment before I realised she meant her

breasts. 'Oh. No. I mean, beautiful. You're beautiful.'

She tossed her head back and tried to laugh but a different sound came out, more like a yelp of pain. And I thought: Oh, you're nervous, too.

I took off my t-shirt. 'There's no prize for this, either.' I pointed at my skinny chest, hairless, toneless, pale. All that basketball had done nothing for my physique. I was a pole, a post.

She smiled at me. 'I like it.' She took off her sweatpants and got into bed.

While she was distracted with arranging the pillows, I slid off my jeans and underpants.

Lying together, she traced with her fingertips the outline of my shoulders, then my arms, pausing to make circles on my skin. 'You have a lot of bruises,' she said.

'Play-off game.'

She put her lips to a few of the bruises and kissed them lightly. Then she sat up and took off her bra. 'Here are my bruises,' she said. She shrugged and wiped her hands under them. 'They get sweaty.'

'Right, I can imagine.'

'Ha ha, what a turn-off I am.'

I touched first one breast, then the other and she closed her eyes. They did feel hot and even clammy. Magically her nipples stiffened.

She turned her bare back and nestled in against me. Then she was reaching behind herself, stroking me. I pushed against her, my hands on her breasts.

'Gentle,' she whispered.

'Sorry.'

She turned to face me again. 'Do you have it?'

I reached out of the bed for my jeans. I held out the condom and she looked at it.

'You think I'm the expert? I can't open the peanuts on planes.' Then she took the condom and straddled me. She inspected the packet carefully, found the tear bit, and took out the condom, giving it a flick with her wrist as if she were shaking a thermometer. Looking earnest, she pulled the condom into place. In that moment, where it gripped me, it was like a tight rubber band on a finger, cutting off circulation. 'That okay?' she said. She was rolling it down forcefully, ensuring it was snug. Then that tight feeling was gone, or it was flooded with other sensations, and though I still sensed I was wearing something, I didn't care. Who cared! She was rubbing herself on me, her eyes closed. I reached up for her breasts. I might have come then, made insane by the very idea of being naked with a girl in her bedroom. I was so so … grateful. Somehow I turned it off in time, the rush. I closed my eyes too. I concentrated on where I was—in Garth's house! Papa Smurf! House of Smurfs! What ugly unappealing toys. I'd lost my job. We'd lost the play-off. I'd lost my sense of self. So many losses! What else? I'd lost my brother! Poor Mikey had never got to be in this position. Probably it had never even occurred to him to be in this position. Loss after loss. Now I was losing my virginity!

Suddenly something hot and close was inside my ear. Keri had bent down and was breathing in it, flicking at it with her tongue. And I was inside her as she moved up and down. Yikes, I could have come right away. I shook her free of my ear. Don't play with fire, lady! She leaned back again, arching her back and bouncing, letting out small gasping sounds in time with her movements. I made the mistake of opening my eyes. Her breasts were going up and down, her mouth was open. Baby, I said aloud, oh, baby. She looked down at me, inquiring. Yes? She was bouncing harder than ever. She stared: *Really?*

She reached behind herself and grabbed me. Where was I? I felt turned inside out, the things that were usually kept safe, trapped, were—where exactly? They were elsewhere, emerging. Retreating. Hello. Now? She stared at me. Angry? Hey! I felt—taller somehow. Even taller. Or fully extended, as if I were expanding beyond my toes, the soles of my feet, the top of my head. Soon I'd strike the walls in both directions, shaking the mirror loose and the lake painting free. Toppling all the Smurfs in the house! She plunged and gripped and stared. I may have been making noises of my own. Her eyes on me were wide. Now already? You think? Hey, you! *Now.*

When she'd come back from the toilet and was in bed, I asked if we could go again.

'You ready?' she said.

Was I? 'Yeah, yeah.'

'You have another condom?'

'Shit. Do you?'

She touched the side of my face with her hand. 'Lying down, you're not tall.'

'I like lying down,' I said.

'This is so much better than Sticky Forest. But you don't get to brag. Or wear the crown. Do you, Ricky?'

'No. This is better.' She didn't need to know about the school assembly.

'Good. I have to go to work, lover. Ugh, I hate that word. Sorry.'

'What shall we call each other?'

'You mean what are our Smurf names?'

'I think you're Bouncy Smurf.'

'Hey!' She hit me on the shoulder. 'Then you're Overeager Smurf.'

Biking home my groin hurt a bit. It was delicious. Auntie Rena was out the front of her house again, smoking. She called out to me and I stopped.

'Always on that bike, Ricky,' she said.

'Can't wait to get my licence,' I said.

'You gotta get out of here, Ricky.'

'I know. Why?'

'Because look at this place.'

'Right. It's really coming along in leaps and bounds. Growing. What's wrong with it?'

'It's disturbing.'

'Yes. In what way?'

She sucked again on her cigarette and blew the smoke away from me. She was wearing a coat but underneath that, who knew. The smoke drifted back into her face, causing her eyes to narrow and giving her that intelligent pissed-off look smokers have.

'You know in the olden days, when I was your age and older, there were two TV channels, if you even know what a TV channel is. And they were both kind of the same. Anyway, that's what this place feels like. There are two channels, with very similar content. Turn the dial further in either direction and all you get is static.'

'But Auntie Rena, you came here to live. You chose here.'

This fact seemed to surprise her. She was looking around, up and down the street. 'Have you noticed the fancy new signs they've put around the lake? Information, maps and everything. They're in two languages. Progress! But te reo isn't one of them. Have you noticed, Ricky?'

I hadn't.

'Turns out Mandarin is what you should be learning. And all the signage up by the fancy new recreation centre? Not a word of te reo. Because it doesn't occur to them. Just doesn't cross their minds. No harm intended. They just don't see it. Such is our beautiful alpine bubble. You breathe this clean air, it's wonderful.' She inhaled through her nostrils. 'But we're up higher and there's not enough oxygen. We're all walking around or running around or cycling around, just a little dizzy. Just a little blank in this thin atmosphere.' She took one last drag, dropped the cigarette butt on the path and stepped on it. 'One thing, Ricky, don't get a motorbike.'

'Why not? Too dangerous?'

'No, I just don't think you'd look good on one.'

'Thanks for the tip, Auntie Rena. By the way, I liked your singing.'

'Oh, that.'

'It was amazing. Dad said so, too.'

'Ha! The man who walked out.'

'He walked out because—'

She cut me off. 'I know why he walked out, honey.'

'To stop himself from crying,' I said.

She looked at me carefully. 'You're a good person, Ricky Clemens.'

Was I? What did my aunt really know about me?

I biked off, gingerly. Would it be easy, for instance, for adults to know I'd had sex? Was that why Rena had told me to get out of Aspiring ASAP? Because I was older now? I'd flipped a switch in my becoming. She saw that in me, did she? She knew. Even though she didn't know. Just like Mr Le Clair. Even though he was just some old St Louis friend of Garth's from a weird time and had a son who played basketball and a car that was the remains of a failed business venture and a chauffeur because maybe he didn't drive—was it as simple as that? Despite all of these explanations, he knew something, didn't he?

Ah, well, maybe here is what he knew: that I was no longer Aspiring's tallest virgin. And that in all but name, I was the new King of Sticky Forest!

*This note is to be handed to the borrower
before each session begins.*

Hello. I am your book. Thank you for borrowing me. Before the book begins, I would like to confirm that I have agreed to be part of the human library. This is completely voluntary and if at any time I feel like stopping the book, I can do so. I would also like to say that my book comes from me. The book may have had help from others in shaping and editing, but these are my thoughts and feelings and the events in the book happened to me. I hope you find this book interesting. Just as with any library, there are a few rules. Other borrowers will be needing this book so please return at the agreed time. The human library project is based around values of respect, inclusiveness, and diversity. Please do not mistreat the book. Please do not interrupt the book. If you have questions or comments, please request time for these after you have returned the book. The book may decide not to answer questions or to engage in any subsequent communication. Please respect this decision. Thank you again—and enjoy!

19.

It was the 30th of October. Blue skies. Not cold. Glassy on the lake. Reflections of the mountains in the watercoloured water. Aspiring at its peak, or one of them.

The spring fair on the reserve land in front of the lake was a calendar highlight. Thousands came from wherever to pat a lamb or eat a lamb or both, no contradiction there, folks. In one pen kids hugged the fluffy bundles while right next door they had them on kebabs. Sometimes it was easier than other times for a vegetarian to embrace his neighbours.

But I'd loved the fair since I was small.

The floats for the pony rides and the trucks and trailers for the mini carnival had been rolling into town throughout the previous day. Hammering came from the carousel. Marquee tents were going up, pathways of awnings. Local stalls selling craft goods, knick-knacks, watercolour paintings, cellophaned baking, hulking great slabs of wooden chopping blocks. And beside them stalls from out of town: a jeweller, a candle maker, a fortune teller, a real estate company. There was a row of farming-related stalls: boots, weatherproof clothes, a place selling Pacific Island holidays. I walked the aisles on my way to the human library.

Our place was a large green canvas tent with its flaps open and a couple of whiteboards from school in front. The whiteboards listed the books: the names of the people and what times they'd be available for borrowing. Fliers were clipped to the boards explaining the project. I'd been asked to help set up but I'd slept in a little and it looked as though most of the work had been done.

'Oh, here he is! Decided to join us, eh?' Johnny stepped out of the tent, carrying two plastic chairs. He threw one at me and I caught it. He came close and said, 'Your shagfest doing you in, Ricky?'

How did he know?

Miss Clarke came from the tent. 'Ricky, perfect timing!' She was trailing a length of paper — A4 sheets stapled together, each bearing a letter and making up our name: The Human Library. She gestured to the entrance of the tent. 'Can you put this up there, please? We have tape but no ladder and I don't want to risk a chair on this grass.' The human ladder.

It was a very slow start. Mostly, people would peer inside the tent, glance at the whiteboards, peer into the tent once more, and walk away. Nah, too weird. Moving on. Miss Milton and Mr Wilson had arrived together for the morning shift. They sat in the tent, chatting, waiting to be borrowed. There were five or six other books also waiting. I recognised a couple of them from around town: a woman who worked in Paper Plus and the guy who ran the lawnmower repair place. Miss Clarke decided we should hand out fliers to passers-by and encourage them to take a shot with a human book.

The first borrowers were two middle-aged women from Dunedin, up for the day, ready to try anything, they said. They chose Miss Milton and the Paper Plus woman and they carried their plastic chairs to spots behind the tent: the 'reading' zone.

Gradually business picked up. I saw Mr Wilson go off a couple of times in quick succession. When he came back the first time, he gave me the thumbs-up.

At one point all the books were out and we started a waiting list of borrowers. The fair was now in full swing and the day was getting hotter. A group of university students came in, five girls with long straight hair. Was it okay if they ate their ice creams while they borrowed a book? And could they all have the same book? Miss Clarke said that wasn't a problem. They disappeared inside the tent and when they came out, two of them had their arms around Auntie Rena. How had she got involved?

'Hi, Ricky!' she said.

I went off to get snacks for the crew and when I came back a fresh lot of books had arrived. There were familiar faces: a few parents of kids at school; Mr Liddell, who owned the Maze; one of the Williams clan who rebuilt war planes; Maeve Munro, who'd been a barefoot waterskiing world champion and still got out on the lake in her seventies.

Sim came by, walking hand-in-hand with Tessa Thompson, Angus's ex, apparently. When had all this happened? Mostly I'd been hanging with Keri at her place. Smurfing when we could. I felt I'd been away for a very long time and had only just returned to a changed place.

'Hi,' I said. 'You come to borrow a book?'

Sim peered into the tent. 'Nah, we're good.' He looked at Tessa. 'We good?'

She nodded.

'You're real good,' I said.

'Yeah,' said Sim. 'You too, bro.'

Then my dad turned up. Of course. Why not? 'What are you doing here?' I said.

'I'm a book,' he said. 'Hello,' he said to Sim and Tessa. He walked past us into the tent.

'He's got a story to tell,' said Sim.

'What story?'

It turned out that Sim had approached him one day at work. 'We settled on his navy days,' said Sim.

'Really?'

'A thing he was involved in. Operation Big Chat.'

'Big Talk,' I said.

'That's the one. Quite cool. Your dad is more than engines and shit, you know.'

'He told you about the operation?'

'At first he didn't think it was much but then we started finding out more and … here he is!'

'You didn't tell me.'

'He wanted it to be a surprise, bro.'

'Huh.'

'Anyway,' he raised Tessa's hand, 'we gotta go. We got hot dogs to eat and rides to ride.'

I went back inside the tent. For a brief moment, until my eyes adjusted to the light, it was all silhouettes. Now I saw that Dad had already been approached by someone. And Maeve Munro's chair was empty, as was Mr War Planes and Mr Maze. Most of the books were out.

In the far corner, someone was waiting. He had his back slightly to me. I looked again.

It was Mr Le Clair.

He turned, saw me, lifted his arm, let it drop. He came over. 'Yes, I'm free. Here's my card.' He handed me the borrowing note we'd written in class.

'When we were working on the arch,' said Mr Le Clair, 'we knew we were doing something very special, right? Is that how it felt to you, Ricky?'

'How do you mean? When I visited it, you mean?'

'No, when we were working on it.'

We were sitting farther away from the tent than the reading zone, at the top of a small slope with a view over the grounds. 'I don't understand,' I said. 'I wasn't working on the arch, just went there with my family. And you, Mr Le Clair—how could you have been working on it? You're not old enough. But maybe you worked there afterwards?'

Mr Le Clair smiled at me. 'Remember topping-out day?'

'Sorry, I don't know what you're talking about.'

'When we had the hoses going.'

'No.'

'And you were looking at the hoses, shaking your head, saying, "I don't know, I don't know." Remember that? They'd built the stand across the way for spectators and it was full, just a huge crowd.'

Listening to this, I felt I was in trouble. But there were people within easy shouting distance. I could call out. Or walk away. 'Afraid not, Mr Le Clair.'

'Call me Tony. I was always Tone. You know.'

'Tone?' I said.

'We had to get the north leg cooled down.'

'South,' I said.

'South, you're right. You had a—what? Eight-foot gap for the keystone.'

'Eight and a half.' You don't challenge mad people. You play along. You agree to their world. It's better that way. I decided then to see how far Le Clair could go.

'Yeah. Whose book is this, Ricky? Eight and a half. But with the thermal expansion that morning, the gap had closed by several inches.'

'Five,' I said. 'It was always going to be tight. I guess no one really knew if it would work.'

'You do something new, that's the way of it. Will it or won't it? I'm pleased you recall it, Ricky.'

'How could I forget, Tone. The vice president was in a helicopter, getting as close as he could to the action. Down below, a Catholic priest and a rabbi saying prayers.' I'd Wiki'ed all of this. It fell from me easily. Sure, I knew this book. Le Clair looked happy.

'Amen. And with that final section, number one hundred and forty-two, swinging into place, hearts in our mouths …'

He must have Wiki'ed it, too. He knew a lot. 'Always going to be touch and go,' I said.

'But the calculations held.'

'We'd stopped work a few times though, through the build,' I said. 'When the ironworkers wanted to know if it was safe. Then the time the tram was stopped from running. Then the protests.'

He studied me. 'I'd forgotten about the protests,' he said. Was this the first crack?

'From the Congress for Racial Equality, remember?' Was I going too far? But he still looked eager. He was grinning. 'They wanted more skilled black workers, more black contractors. Said we were building a symbol of discrimination.'

He slapped his thigh. Yes! Remembering. Pretending to remember. 'Then the walk-offs from the plumbers,' he said.

'The plumbers?' Now it was my turn—I didn't know about any plumbers, did I?

'In the visitor centre,' he said. 'They didn't want to work with the black plumbers. Nothing to do with race, they said. Just that the black plumbers were used to working for lower wages and they didn't want a part of that.'

Who are you?

'Still,' he said. 'We got there. Late and over budget but we made it.'

I nodded. My mouth felt dry, sticky. The fear was back.

Le Clair said, 'It wasn't a *thing* we were building, or it was a thing, made of concrete and steel, but it was also an idea, a beautiful idea. They take longer.'

'Eero Saarinen,' I said quietly. 'He never got to see it.'

'But at least he had the idea,' said Le Clair, leaning forward. 'He saw it in his mind. Ahead of everyone, he had it in his mind. The mind, Ricky, is a house of countless rooms.'

What room were we in now?

We looked out across the fair towards the lake, where three hot-air balloons had appeared, seeming to hang motionless above the mountains. The balloons somehow lifted me, but not pleasantly, as if I were up there with them suddenly. There was a burst of noise in my ears—from? From the balloon's gas fire as it worked to retain its height? *Whoosh.* I rushed to the top of my head. Le Clair wasn't mad. He saw things! He saw inside me. Le Clair. Le Clear. Clear-sighted! I hated him. I swallowed and my ears popped and I was coming down again.

I said, 'Why did you track me down here?'

'There are only thirteen of us,' he said. 'I just like to keep tabs on the arch chapter.'

'They took my brother already.'

They? Who were they? The creatures who sent Le Clair?

'I know,' said Le Clair.

'They crushed my parents.'

'Your parents have you.'

'They remain crushed.'

'But look at you. You're just getting bigger and bigger.'

'When will that stop?'

'I don't control that.'

'Who does?'

He looked at his watch. 'We're over time, I think. This book is due back in the library.'

'Are you really an old friend of Garth's?'

He shrugged, looking up at the balloons. 'Don't care for those things.'

I said, 'He believes he met you in a group for men whose wives died.'

'People believe things that are good for them to believe.'

'He believes things that are good for you to have him believe.'

He stood and picked up his plastic chair. For a moment, the silver tips of his string tie hung down and I had a sudden wish to grab them and pull them tight against his narrow throat. I could do that, couldn't I? Loom over him. Loom and threaten and make him small. He was small. I was massive, uncontainable.

'You know,' he said, 'they flew a hot-air balloon one time through the arch.'

I didn't know about this. Was it true? Probably. But I could scarcely concentrate on what he was saying now.

'This was in the seventies. They got permission, thought they could do it, and they clipped the side. Fell something like seventy feet before they got control and pulled up. Could have been a real mess.'

'Are they in the arch chapter of the Halfway to Hell club? The people in the balloon, are you keeping tabs on them?'

'The club is construction only. Maybe someone else has another club, I don't know.'

'But how does it all work?' I said. 'And why? You almost die, you were *supposed* to die, and then at some point you have to pay the price or someone in your family does? Because you *owe* the universe a life? Is that it? Because someone—God?—is keeping tabs, doing the maths? It's nuts! The people who cheat death in car accidents, they have to prematurely cough up a life at some point? Someone in the Saker family is going to pay the price for the fact Hamish and his father pulled through that crash? People who come back from heart attacks? Near drownings? Strokes? Clubs for all of them, tabs for all of them? You survive but there's a cost? Tit for tat? Eye for an eye? Karma? What are the rules here? I like consistency in my fantasy worlds, you know? Explain please.'

Le Clair held up his hands. 'Ricky, this book may decide not to answer questions or to engage in any subsequent communication. Please respect this decision.'

Then it hit me: Maybe I did know who and what he was.

'Mr Le Clair,' I said, 'here's the deal. The facts as we know them. I'm just some freaky kid from the fifth-most-popular town in the Central Lakes region. You know I'm just Ricky Clemens, almost sixteen, just got a girlfriend. Average basketballer. Former restaurant worker. Noncommittal vegetarian. Worried about the future of the planet, our warming lake, our retreating glaciers, our disappearing insects. Over-tall and unsure of where he's ending, where he'll end up, where anything and everything will end up. Had a grandfather who worked on the arch. Had an older brother who was killed in a car accident, which changed everything.

That's me. That's who I am. I have loops going around in my head, stuff I make up. Where I'm the star or I've got to figure something out, find something, locate someone. Always sifting clues. You, Mr Le Clair, are one of those loops. My parents are stuck in their own loop. People get stuck. There are loops and loops. You came in on one and I'm having trouble getting rid of you. And this stupid idea about how the universe works? Tit for tat? One life for another. Mine too, my idea. I made it up. Because it's better than thinking it's all a bunch of accidents, right? There's got to be a pattern. Sense. It's better than knowing we all live on this edge, on the shore of this lake, and that we're here for a time far shorter than the life of the stone we skip across the water, which sinks and is never seen again. How to leave the loop, how to disappear you, that's proving difficult. But that's who you are.'

I was exhausted, my head spinning.

You're my anxiety talking.

His eyes narrowed. 'You're diagnosing yourself now, Ricky?'

'I think this is what's going on.'

'You don't sound too sure.'

'I'm not.' I stared hard at his thin slice of half nose. It seemed in a worse state than ever, almost visibly crumbling. I said, 'I think I made you up. But see—parts of you are crumbling. *Look, you're falling apart! I'm unmaking you, dude! Just like that ludicrous car you drive—you're getting shorter and shorter!*'

For a moment he seemed caught. His right hand moved in the direction of his nose, as if about to check it was still in place. Then he dropped his hand again and picked up the chair.

He was walking back in the direction of the tent but now he turned. 'Hey, Ricky, where's your pin by the way? Your Gateway Arch pin.'

'I don't have a pin.'

'Maybe you got it when you visited.'

'I got a baseball cap when I visited St Louis.'

'Huh.' He had his back to me again, moving away.

'I wore it till it wore out.'

'Okay,' he said.

'You have the pin. I don't.'

He spoke over his shoulder and the words were hard to make out. 'Today, Ricky, there will be a tragedy.'

'What?' I called out. 'What did you say?' But he was gone.

I took off on my bike after the conversation with Mr Le Clair. I had no idea where to go, what to do. I went hard. I went for a PB. Tore around the southern side of the lake in the direction of Heaphy Falls. Through certain technical dips and twists on the track, I went faster than I'd ever gone before, not bothering to brake. When I stopped I'd come out by the inlet. This was where they set out for the island in swimming races. I threw my bike down and sat on the stones, breathing hard. It was deserted. Everyone was at the fair. I scanned the shore. Nothing. Even the birds had gone. Good.

Then my eye caught something. A small mound in the distance, about halfway between me and the water. Maybe a pile of lakeweed or a tangle of sticks. I stood up but couldn't make out what it was. I walked towards it. Soon I saw that it was a neat pile of clothes anchored by a pair of running shoes. I looked out across the lake. No one. This wasn't unusual. Long-distance swimmers went out for ages. I crouched beside the clothes and waited. It was a nice day for a swim.

This was also the spot where the university student had set

off for the party on the island on his useless craft and never made it and was never found.

Today there will be a tragedy.

Le Clair's words hung about.

I looked at my phone. How long should I wait before calling the police? But the owner of the clothes was probably just on the far side of the island, turning for home, having a good training session.

I stood up and walked to the water's edge.

Far off in the direction of the northern arm, a small boat was bouncing gently on the lake, most likely doing a spot of fishing. Back in the direction of town, there was more activity, with kayakers closer in and farther out, a few boats pulling skiers. In between the fishing boat and the town, a wide empty expanse of calm purplish water.

Then way off to my left, I thought I saw something. Not in the water but on the shore, moving in my direction. The sun was shining into my eyes and, even shielding them, I couldn't be sure of what I was seeing. For a moment it looked like some weird bird with a large beaky head and thin black legs. The bird of the apocalypse! The beak swivelled and the bird seemed to stagger before regaining its position and walking forward. When the sun shifted I saw what it was: a man in a wetsuit carrying a kayak on his head.

He wasn't going into the lake but towards me. When he was close enough, I waved. He paused, lifting the kayak higher above his head for a better view.

'Clemens!'

It was Coach Dennett.

'You guarding my stuff?'

'That's right,' I said.

'Good man.' He put the kayak down and bent over, catching

his breath. Then he reached for a water bottle, which was hooked onto his belt, and drank. 'Ironman,' he said. 'Two months away. If I'm not dead before then. What are you doing here anyway? Should be at the fair.'

'Taking a break.'

'Righto.'

We both looked out across the lake, stuck for something to say. All of our previous conversations were to do with basketball. That seemed far off now. And who wanted to bring up our failed campaign?

'So,' Coach finally said, 'you'll be back again for another season next year?'

'Yep,' I said. Was that true?

'That's the spirit.' He bent down, shook one of his running shoes, and caught his watch as it fell out. 'I don't think we've tapped even fifty percent of who you are, Ricky, and who you can become.'

A great surge went through me when he said that. If he hadn't crouched at that moment to pick up his micro towel, and in crouching let out a sharp wet fart, I might have collapsed in tears.

'Whoops,' he said.

Coach was starting to peel off the top of his wetsuit so I picked up my bike and said goodbye.

Keri came to the human library in the afternoon. She pressed an envelope into my hand and whispered, 'Happy early birthday.' She looked at me again. 'You okay?'

'Not sure,' I said.

I shook the envelope. 'Can I open it now?'

'You have to. I mean, it hasn't got any embarrassing declarations inside or anything.'

'Oh.' I felt that as a sudden punch. She saw it, too, and winced as if she'd been struck as well.

'Told you I was shit at this,' she said.

I pulled out a voucher of some kind. It took me a moment to work out what it was for. 'Okay.' I stared again at the voucher.

'It's for two,' she said.

'You mean …?'

She laughed. 'I'm struggling with your enthusiasm. And your gratitude.'

We joined a queue of tourists and visitors at the parasailing place on the lakefront. They had three boats out and we were told the wait wouldn't be too long. I was ready to bolt at any moment. I had the feeling Keri was only pretending. It was some kind of test for me. Why did she want to do it? And why did she think I'd want to do it? Wasn't it a prank present? At any moment she'd jump out of the queue and laugh and say, What the hell are you lining up here for? But still she waited, shielding her eyes and looking up into the sky as if she was already dreaming of being up there.

'Maybe I won't fit in the boat,' I said. 'If there's a height restriction.'

'What are you talking about? There's just going to be sky above you. No roof. You won't bump your head. How tall do you think you are?'

'I haven't measured today.'

Keri reached up with her arm and patted my head. 'I can still do that.'

'This is way too expensive. Maybe we can get a refund.'

'Stop ruining my present.'

When we got to the front of the queue, Kathy Wang took our tickets. She'd been speaking Chinese to a couple ahead of us.

'Ni chi le ma?' said Keri.

Kathy said, 'Chi le.'

'Wo shi, Keri.' Keri held out her hand and Kathy shook it.

'Wo shi, Kathy. Ni shi tade nupengyou ma?'

Keri looked at me. 'Yexu!'

They both laughed.

'Okay,' I said. 'That was obviously very funny.'

Then Keri said something else quickly that Kathy didn't understand. 'I only learned for four years.'

'Oh,' said Kathy. 'Your accent is pretty good.'

'Not really,' said Keri. 'You got a good gig in this town, eh.'

'All the work I want,' said Kathy. 'I just have to pretend to be Chinese. You know, more than I am.' She took our tickets and pointed to the boat that had pulled up. 'That's your one. Have fun!'

We walked to the boat. 'I didn't know you spoke Chinese,' I said.

'But, Ricky, you don't know anything much about me.'

That was true. What was her life like in Auckland? Ubers, Uber Eats, sex? I'd never been, except to the airport. A fact pinged to the surface. 'Auckland is like twenty percent Asian, right?' But she wasn't listening or chose not to hear. She was taking her shoes and socks off, putting them in her shoulder bag. I slipped off my sneakers. 'I don't have a bag,' I said.

The guy in the boat was reaching for our stuff. 'Tandem? You want to go up together? Climb in and we'll get you sorted.'

He stood in knee-deep water, clipping us into the seat and securing the harness of the parachute. He explained the process.

How we'd start off gently, pulling away from the shore, and once we were out in the lake with some speed on, he'd release us and we'd go up gradually. Did we have any questions? No? Good. Then he was behind us, making sure the chute was okay. He climbed back into the boat and turned on the engine.

'Shit,' I said.

'What?' said Keri.

'I'm scared of heights.'

She laughed. Then she stared at me. 'You can't be scared of heights. You *are* the heights. You walk around at height.'

I'd never had a problem looking out of tall buildings or off the sides of bridges. That was my dad. But now … 'It's just come on.'

'Just this minute?'

'Yeah. I don't know if I can do this.' I closed my eyes and saw myself falling. I was slipping from the shiny silver sides of … I opened them again at once. We rocked backwards slightly as the boat accelerated away from the shore.

Today there will be a tragedy.

'I think you can do this,' she said.

'You're not me.'

'I'm here.' She took my hand, gripped it hard. 'You know in Chinese, the word for landscape is shanshui. Mountains plus water.' With a finger, she traced a shape on the back of my hand.

'What's that?' I said.

'That's the Chinese character. The three drops for water, then the three lines for the peaks of the mountain.'

'If I drew a picture of someone throwing up, would that be the Chinese word for terrified?'

I went to stand up but then I was pushed back as the boat started pulling harder. Fins of wake carved up its sides, lightly splashing us. The guy looked our way and Keri gave him the thumbs-up. The noise of the boat was louder now. I shouted at her, 'Why'd you give him the thumbs-up?'

She shouted back, 'You wanna stop? I can get him to stop. No worries.'

The harness had pressure on it now. The wind caught Keri's hair, blowing it off her face. 'I can tell him, Ricky!'

The guy looked at us again. He pointed upwards. Sky time! He pulled a lever.

'Arghh!' Someone was shouting in my ear.

It was me.

'Arghhhh!'

We lifted suddenly away from the boat, hanging for a moment, my feet dangling in the water. Then we were lifting higher. Keri was squeezing my hand. I felt her looking at me but I had to keep staring ahead.

I thought all my internal organs—heart, liver, lungs, all the curly piping and soft shapes and lumps—would become visible on my outside. And ... weirdest feeling: you could fry me! Fry the vegetarian! Garth in the kitchen at Pete's could slice me with his precious knives and set me sizzling in a pan. All my bits tightening on the heat, browning and spitting. Why not? All of us were returning eventually to ...

Keri's mouth was close to my ear. It was easier to hear now. Quiet almost. 'Isn't this, you know, beautiful? Isn't it?'

I'd had my eyes closed. They opened, as if by themselves. Finally, I looked around. I looked down.

'Yes,' I said. I nodded. 'Yes.'

We were circling above the lake, swinging gently in the air, now with a view back to our township.

We could see the marquee tents of the fair and the lakefront road with a long line of traffic. Farther back, the brown scars in the land where the big development was going in, shapes that must have been bulldozers, diggers. The shiny silver rectangles of the new supermarket and the recreation centre. The green of the golf course, the sandy eyes of the bunkers. Rows of roofs. Trees. The small people, getting smaller.

Keri said, 'Is this how we look to you?'

'Welcome to my world,' I said.

She shook her hand free of mine. I realised I'd been holding it very tightly. Turned out she hadn't been holding my hand; I'd had hers in a vice.

'Hope my fingers still work,' she said.

'Sorry.'

We were drifting in a new direction now, angling towards the head of the lake and the mountains. Could we peek over them?

A gust caught us and we rolled over it in our floaty seat. Whoosh! It was the same acceleration I'd felt when speaking to Le Clair at the human library, except this was clean and exhilarating. At the peak of the wind wave, I craned my long neck and thought I saw a flash of sea beyond the mountains. The other side! I thought I saw my life then, the future, leaving Aspiring, aspiring. Aspiring to what? No one I knew was there in this future. I'd left everyone behind. Mum, Dad, Auntie Rena, Sim and Johnny, even Keri. It was terrifying. I couldn't wait.

But maybe I would never leave Le Clair behind. I would have to find a way to—what? Not get rid of him. That wasn't it. *Own* him. Ownership, Clemens! Coach's words from the locker room came back. They remained mysterious. I didn't have a clue up here in the control tower.

Then we dipped, turned again, westward, in the direction of Garth's house, Smurf HQ.

'This is cool,' I said into Keri's ear.

She was grinning. 'Oh, yeah, it's okay, I suppose.'

Slowly we began to lose height. I looked down into the water of the lake, the different shades, lighter and darker, blue and green and grey as though someone couldn't make up their mind painting it. Things were moving on the water's surface, painting the light—these were the shadows of high clouds in the blue sky. Our boat circled and was now heading for the shore, letting us down along a gentle column of air.

Soon my dangling feet were dipped in the lake.

'Too soon!' said Keri. 'Too soon! Why does everything end too soon?'

Yes, endings. But I was thinking of something else: beginnings!

20.

We sit at the kitchen table, eating dinner, exhausted from the fair. It is too strange. No arguments, no prayers, no nothing. Have they both forgotten the date? It's all pretty pleasant and unreal. Mum and Dad chat about nothing much. The weather! How lucky it was to have such a nice day for the human library. How Dad was one of the most popular books. He was always on loan throughout the day.

'If you were an actual book,' I say, 'you'd be really dog-eared and beaten-up and have pages missing.'

'That's pretty much how I feel,' he says. He sips his beer. 'You know for next time —'

'Next time!' says Mum. 'Listen to him.'

'Oh, surely you'll be doing it again, Ricky?'

'Next time,' I say, 'I think Mum is a book.'

'Great idea!' says Dad.

'I could never compete with Mr Popularity,' she says.

'What would you tell?' I say. 'What's your book about?'

'There's nothing,' she says. 'Really. Nothing at all you'd want to get a stranger to listen to.'

'That's not true,' says Dad.

Then Mum stands up to clear the plates.

'You could tell about your grandfather,' Dad says. 'The arch.'

'Not my story,' says Mum. 'No. I wouldn't tell that one, although he was an amazing man.' She is waiting over the table, not ready or able to move. She wants to say something. Finally she says, 'Ah, well, Mikey would have been twenty-one.'

Dad looks at her and reaches for her hand. 'That's true,' he says. And they both smile at me.

I feel as though I can't breathe.

I go upstairs and take Mike's softball glove out of the drawer. I put it on, then I put the glove over my face. Again.

I think, I must look weird. I must look like I don't have a face. But I do have a face. This one. In here.

Inside the glove it's dark. The beautiful sweet leather smell. Like toffee and varnish. I give it a lick. Okay, it doesn't taste great. When I kissed Keri, the astonishing taste of another person's mouth! Why hadn't anyone told me about that? Tongues.

I remembered myself with the glove. When I was younger … You could yell into the glove and hardly any sound came out. It was as though you were at the end of a long corridor and the little slits between the fingers were windows splintering the light. I'd done it plenty of times before—the muted yelling. Small boy inside a glove. But tonight, no. I take the glove off my face.

My phone pings. Keri.

> you are my fave human librarian
> you have borrowed my heart
> want it back any time soon?
> you can renew any time
> wassup with olds? you okay?
> olds are weird and good. i'm okay
> big night for you all. take caringest care of each other
> we are. PS: I want to carry on READING you

you'll go blind

i'll go crazy

i'll go halves

game of two halves

me game

me tarzan

night night big boy

howling at the moon

I stared at my phone for a while. Should I or shouldn't I?

you won't leave aspiring soon tho eh

not soon not soon but ...

those three dots scare me

me too me two we two don't be scared

When I get off my bed, I accidentally knock the glove to the floor and I bend down to scoop it up. Oh, bending, ye lost art! Oh, life ahead of physios and chiros, of acupuncture and healing hands! Gravity's revenge on the too-tall.

Something catches my eye on the carpet, behind one of the legs of my bedside drawers. Just a flash. I peer closer. It's small and silvery. I reach for it, flick it forward with my finger, then pick it up. I hold it in my palm.

It's a pin of the Gateway Arch.

Downstairs I say to my dad, 'Coming out for some throws?'

'Oh, not right now,' he says. He's slumped in front of the TV. Cricket. Suddenly the day's exertions have worked their way into his system. He looks incredibly tired. Older. Cricket, croquet—it's only a few letters different and then he'll be slumped in a chair at the Aspiring Lifestyle retirement village. How many years before he'll be looking through the window at all the furious one-hand-gloved golfers destroying their clubs? Plenty, I guess. Though right now it feels suddenly closer. And if he found any errant balls in his garden, would he give them back? Like hell.

'What about you, Mum?' I say.

'Me?' She's wiping down the table.

'Come out for some throws.'

'Her?' says my dad. 'She can't throw.'

'Well, that's not true,' she says.

'Come out then,' I say. 'I feel like throwing. Don't you? Loosening the old arm. We haven't had throws in so long.'

She looks out the window. The day is already losing the light. 'It's a nice evening,' she says.

'It's gorgeous,' I say. 'Aspiring at its best!'

I have my old catcher's mitt by my side. Mike's glove is back in the glass cabinet. I put it there. I say, 'Come on, old people. Are you both too old to come out and play?'

It's still warm, the night air a light covering on the bare skin of my arms and legs. I squat down in our back garden and punch the glove. 'Toss it in, Mum. Give it all you've got.' I haven't been in this pose for a long time but it comes back. It comes flooding back.

'All I've got? Be careful what you ask for, buddy.'

'Wind that arm back and throw it as hard as you can!'

'You know,' she says, 'the golf swing is like throwing a ball. Same principle. Same pressure shift in the feet. Same right arm movement. Same finish. Wind it up and let the body come along with the relaxed wrists, the easy arms. No tension.'

'Yeah, yeah,' I say, 'the lady talks a big game but has she got it?'

My dad has come to the open ranchslider in his bare feet.

He's grinning, rubbing his tattoo. He stretches and yawns. Maybe soon he'll be taking the ball from Mum and giving me some throws. He used to do it when I played, when he wanted me to be better. Oh, yes, he's itching to take over. When he rubs his tat, that means gimme gimme gimme. He's got a hard throw and he doesn't much care that you're a kid, a giant kid.

'You ready for this?' says Mum.

'Do it,' says my dad. 'Give it heaps!'

'I've been ready for years,' I say.

She winds her arm way back and lifts her front foot as if she's a baseball pitcher.

'Wrong sport,' says my dad. He's laughing. 'Wrong sport!'

She pauses mid-throw, her front foot raised. 'What?' she shouts.

'You're doing it wrong!'

'I'm doing it wrong?'

'Yeah!'

Then she throws the ball. In a beautiful powerful motion, she hurls it.

Maybe I closed my eyes for a split second. Not because I was afraid. But because … when you close your eyes, you're taking a picture of what you've just seen, right? You're keeping it safe. Click. The night my mum sent down the pitch, watched by my dad, who was laughing. Thirtieth of October. Aspiring. As if this was the new thing we did now on this special date. We convened in the back garden on a warm spring evening, filled with the stories of our fellow humans, dreaming of other stories, and threw balls at each other with all our might. We remembered in this way and we went a little crazy.

How did that pin get into my room?

How did Keri decide to like me?

I don't know where that ball went that my mum threw. Nowhere near me and my outstretched glove. Into the neighbours! Yes. Must have passed through the hedge with barely a whistle or a rustle. A clean passage, as if it wasn't just passing through physical space but time as well. That ball had some speed. Hey, Mike, hey Mikey, you should have seen it.

We all paused. All of the human library stopped chattering, stopped reading and speaking and listening and sharing. It was completely quiet. Then through the hedge the neighbour's dog was barking, very excited. Then he stopped, too. Silence. He had the ball in his mouth, I suppose. Come here, boy. Come here. Good boy.

There we were, in no great hurry to resume, waiting for the ball to come back to us.

Would it come back to us?

What had happened to it?

Then it occurred to me that I could easily walk to the hedge and simply look over it to find the answer. And that is exactly what I did. I had the power.

Acknowledgments

Thanks to Carol and Ross for their kindness and generosity. I'm also grateful to Victoria University of Wellington for support during the writing of this book. This novel is dedicated to the memory of my friend, James Hughes, also known as Archie, whom I first met in St Louis in 1990. James was a precious person and a wildly talented storyteller.

About the author

Damien Wilkins has published novels, collections of short stories, and a book of poems. He has written for television and theatre. He also writes and records his own songs as The Close Readers. His work has won several awards, including a New Zealand Book Award. He lives in Wellington, where he is the director of the International Institute of Modern Letters at Victoria University.

About Annual Ink

Annual Ink is a children's imprint within Massey University Press. The imprint's editors, Susan Paris and Kate De Goldi, seek out and work closely with mostly new writers and artists—a model they established when making *Annual* (2016) and *Annual 2* (2017). In partnership with MUP, and in the spirit of the Annuals, they aim to help create and publish high-quality and innovative books across a variety of forms, primarily for middle readers.

www.annualink.com

ANNUALink

Annual Ink is an imprint of Massey University Press
First published in 2020 by Massey University Press
Private Bag 102904, North Shore Mail Centre
Auckland 0745, New Zealand
www.masseypress.ac.nz

Text copyright © Damien Wilkins, 2020

Design by Marcus Thomas
Cover design by Ross Murray

Page 139: Lyrics from 'Loyal', words and music by Dave
Dobbyn © Copyright Native Tongue Music Publishing Ltd.
All print rights administered in Australia and New Zealand
by Hal Leonard Australia Pty Ltd ABN 13 085 333 713.
www.halleonard.com.au. Used by permission. All rights
reserved. Unauthorised reproduction is illegal.

The moral right of the author has been asserted

All rights reserved. Except as provided by the Copyright
Act 1994, no part of this book may be reproduced, stored
in or introduced into a retrieval system or transmitted in any
form or by any means (electronic, mechanical, photocopying,
recording or otherwise) without the prior written permission
of both the copyright owner(s) and the publisher.

A catalogue record for this book is available from the
National Library of New Zealand

Printed and bound in China by Everbest Investment Ltd

ISBN: 978-0-9951229-4-9

The assistance of Creative New Zealand is gratefully
acknowledged by the publisher

ARTS COUNCIL OF NEW ZEALAND TOI AOTEAROA